Sassy

The Dazzle Disaster
Dinner Party

Books by Sharon M. Draper

Sassy #1: Little Sister Is Not My Name
Sassy #2: The Birthday Storm
Sassy #3: The Silver Secret
Sassy #4: The Dazzle Disaster Dinner Party

For a complete list of Sharon Draper's books,
please visit www.sharondraper.com.

Sassy

The Dazzle Disaster
Dinner Party

Sharon M. Draper

SCHOLASTIC PRESS
New York

This book is dedicated to Mary Rose Draper,
who loves to cook and share
great food with her friends

Library of Congress Cataloging-in-Publication Data Available

ISBN 978-0-545-07154-3

10 9 8 7 6 5 4 3 2 1   10 11 12 13 14

Printed in the U.S.A.   23
First edition, October 2010

Book design by Elizabeth B. Parisi

CHAPTER ONE

The Mystery Limousine

"**W**ow! Take a look at that!" I exclaim.

"I can't believe it!" Jasmine whispers.

"Slick, man!" Travis says. He looks really impressed.

"Awesome!" Carmelita echoes.

"I've honestly never seen anything like it!" I tell my friends. I don't think they have, either.

"Not at an ordinary school like ours," Holly adds.

What we are looking at is a long, black, shiny limousine. It is pulling up to the front door of our school. It gleams in the morning sunlight. Most kids arrive in dusty, plain cars. The limo looks like a bright black diamond next to the crayon-yellow school bus that pulls up behind it.

The bus unloads noisy students. All of them are dressed in our school's blue-and-white uniforms. But they get real quiet as they look and point at the sleek black car waiting in the school's driveway. We wait for the bell to ring so we can go inside to class. But no one wants that to happen yet. We are all really, really curious about the mysterious car.

The limousine just sits there. No doors open.

We wait impatiently to see who might step out of such a glorious car.

"You think it's a princess?" Holly asks hopefully.

"What kind of princess would want to go to our plain old school?" I ask.

"Maybe it's a sultan!" Basima suggests.

"Princes and sultans and royalty like that are only in fairy tales," Rusty says.

"Not true. There are two real live princes who live in England," Jasmine tells him with authority. "And one day one of them will be the king of England! For real!"

We all nod in agreement. The car still does not move. The doors still do not open.

"Why don't you go over there and peek in the window, Princess?" Josephina suggests. "After all, your real name is Princess!"

Princess shakes her head. "My mother named me that because she thought it was a pretty name. But neither my mom or me has ever even *touched* a limo!"

"Maybe it's the president's daughters!" Holly says hopefully. "Maybe the limo is full of Secret Service people!"

"And why would the president's kids want to visit our school?" I ask them.

Nobody has a good answer.

Carmelita scrunches up her face in thought. "It *could* be a movie star or a famous singer hiding in there," she says finally. "Maybe we're going to have a surprise concert that the teachers didn't tell us about."

"Maybe," Jasmine says slowly. "Remember when your grandmother came to our school, Sassy? She is a famous storyteller and she did a surprise presentation for all the kids."

I laugh a little. "Yes, but my grammy arrived in our dirty old brown car. She's really cool, but she's no rock star. I'm not sure if she ever rode in a limo, either."

"I wish they'd just open the door so we can quit guessing," Carmelita says with a sigh.

"I wonder what she looks like," Misty says.

"Who says it's a girl?" Travis responds. "It could be a rich boy inside."

"You think the kid inside is rich?" I ask.

"I guess you'd have to have some cash to drive to school in a limousine," Holly tells her.

"If it's a girl, I bet she won't have anything as cool as your Sassy Sack," Jasmine tells me. All the girls around me nod in agreement.

I laugh. "She probably has a golden leather designer purse instead!"

I carry what I call my Sassy Sack every single day — my wonderful, beautifully shiny shoulder bag. It's purple and silver and pink and magenta. It has a long strap, several outside compartments with buttons and zippers, and lots of little hidden pockets inside.

It has diamond-looking sparkly things all over it, and when I'm outside and the sunlight hits it just right, it really shines.

Even I'm not sure what's in there, but I know when I reach down into it, I always seem to find exactly what I need.

I dig into my Sassy Sack and pull out a small bag of jelly beans and a pair of mini binoculars.

I offer the candy to my friends, and I put the binoculars up to my eyes. But the limo has tinted glass all around. All I can see through the lenses is a limo that looks bigger and shinier up close.

"Love those cherry Jelly Bellies, Sassy," Travis says as he gobbles a handful of candy. "Thanks." He takes a few more jelly beans, then asks, "Can you see behind the tinted glass?"

"I'd need X-ray vision for that, Travis!" I tell him with a

laugh. I offer him the binoculars, but he says he can't see anything, either.

The front door of the school opens then, and our principal, Mrs. Bell, hurries out. She's touching her hair, I guess to make sure it looks okay. She goes to the driver's side of the limousine.

The tinted window slides down, but we can see nothing from where we are standing. We can't even hear what is being said, only a deep male voice. Then we hear a faint, high-pitched laugh from Mrs. Bell. She has a squeaky voice. When she speaks, it's almost like listening to fingernails on a blackboard. But this morning we can't even hear that very clearly.

It's driving me crazy!

The window slides back up, and Mrs. Bell hurries back into the building. I check my watch, which has a band covered with purple sparkles. The bell is late. All the students still wait outside, whispering about the mystery limousine at our front door.

But no doors open. No bell rings.

"What was that all about?" I whisper to Jasmine.

She shrugs. "This is big, Sassy. I think we're about to be famous or something."

"You think?" Holly adds.

"Maybe they're waiting for the news crew to arrive so when the princess gets out, they will be on hand to take her picture," Travis suggests.

But no news reporters and photographers come screeching around the corner. Everything is unusually quiet.

Finally, Rusty calls out, "Hey, look! I think the driver's door is opening!"

Slowly, from the darkness of the car, a tall, slim man in a gray uniform slides from the front seat. He walks to one of the back doors and then waits there. He does not look at us at all.

I hold my breath. I think all the rest of the kids are inhaling as well.

The driver then speaks into a cell phone. We cannot make out most of what he says, but finally we hear him say clearly, "Yes, sir!" in a real loud voice. A couple of us jump back in surprise.

We strain to see who's in the backseat of the limo, but the driver blocks our view as he opens the door.

He offers his hand to the person who slowly emerges. She takes his hand for just a second, then pushes it away, as if to say, "I can do this by myself!"

She is petite and dainty, and she looks like she's probably in third or fourth grade — just like us!

She has straight black hair that's almost as glossy as

the wax on the car. She's dressed not in a blue-and-white uniform but in a really pretty pink dress and matching pink shoes.

She does not turn her head to look at any of us as she walks next to the driver. She just looks straight ahead. She does not smile.

I think she looks a little scared.

Mrs. Bell meets them at the school entrance and whisks the new girl and the driver inside.

We are left outside with even more questions.

"She's pretty," Carmelita says.

"I wonder where she's from," Holly wonders.

"That guy who brought her here is clearly not her father. Where are her parents, I wonder," Misty muses.

"How do you know he's not her dad?" I ask.

"A daddy would have held her hand or whispered something to make her laugh," Jasmine says.

"Yeah. That guy was following orders from somebody at the other end of that cell phone," says Holly.

"She's about our age," Carmelita observes.

"Do rich kids have to wear uniforms like the rest of us? Or will she get to wear cute outfits every day?" I ask the others.

"And will she arrive in a limo every day?" Jasmine asks.

"I wonder what class they will put her in," Rusty says.

"We don't even know for sure if she is enrolling at our school yet," I tell them.

The driver emerges then, without the new girl, and swiftly gets back into the big black car. He drives away with a whoosh. The school driveway looks really empty all of a sudden.

The morning bell finally rings, and we troop inside to find out more about the mysterious new student.

CHAPTER TWO

The New Girl

Even though our school is not fancy enough for kids to show up in limousines every day, I really like it. My classes are fun and my teachers make me feel special.

My English teacher's name is Miss Armstrong. She's also our homeroom teacher, and every morning she reminds us, "Fourth grade is the best!" Of course, every teacher says that every year. I think it's something they learn in teacher school.

When Miss Armstrong reads to us, her voice reminds me of saxophone music. It's deep and rich and pretty. Her voice makes words sound like they're dancing on fluttering leaves, all magical and mysterious. I don't tell my friends stuff like that, however. I think they just hear ordinary words when Miss Armstrong speaks.

Miss Armstrong kinda looks like a saxophone, too. She's thin at the top and curved at the bottom. She smells like tangerines. I've seen the citrus lotion in her top desk drawer.

"Good morning, Sassy and Jasmine!" she says as the two of us walk into the classroom.

"Hi, Miss Armstrong," we reply.

But we are not paying much attention to our teacher. Because sitting in the second row, right next to my desk, is the new girl! She is reading a book. Her head is down and she does not look up as the rest of the class noisily enters the room. Strange.

The class gets unusually quiet very quickly — even before the final sit-down bell rings. I can hear the whispers of a few kids.

"How come she doesn't have to wear a uniform like we do?"

"How old is she?"

"What's up with the limousine and driver?"

No one seems to have any answers. Only lots of questions. So we all find our seats and wait.

The bell rings.

Miss Armstrong stands in front of the room near her desk. She smiles like she's really excited and says, "Good morning, class! I know that many of you were outside this morning and wondered about the arrival of our newest student."

I want to ask a million questions, but I wait for her to continue.

"Please let me introduce Miss Lillian Ling!"

All eyes turn to the girl in pink. She looks at the teacher. Then, very slowly, she turns her head and looks around. She gives me a teeny, tiny smile, then looks down again.

Miss Armstrong continues. "It might not be easy for Lillian to adjust to our school, so please give her some time. I'm sure she will welcome your friendship. Now, open your spelling books to page eighty-seven."

"Can't we ask any questions about the new girl?" Travis blurts out.

"No, you can't, Travis. Not unless information about her is contained on page eighty-seven of your spelling book!"

Travis frowns but says nothing else. The spelling lesson continues.

Lillian continues to read her book as if none of us exist. Not even the teacher.

By lunchtime I've observed several things about Lillian. I make a list of the most noticeable.

1. Her backpack looks brand-new. It's got pink sparkles on it. I like it.
2. Her pencils are freshly sharpened. They are also pink.

3. She writes down most of what Miss Armstrong says in a shiny rose-colored notebook.
4. She doesn't raise her hand even one time to answer a question.
5. She never looks at any of us.
6. She stays in the room while the rest of us go on a bathroom break.
7. She looks like she would rather be anyplace else than here with us.

Her desk is next to mine, so I notice lots of things close up.

8. Even though her fingernails are painted with pale pink gloss, it looks like she bites them.
9. Her hands shake when she digs into her book bag for paper or pens.
10. She looks like she's very close to crying.

The bell rings for lunchtime. Usually, my friends and I hurry into the hot, crowded cafeteria together. We pick up our disposable trays, get a cheeseburger, a little cup of fruit, a juice box, and head to a table where mostly fourth graders are squeezed together.

I like when Travis sits with us. He makes us laugh. He

slurps spaghetti and sucks Jell-O cubes into his mouth from the plate. He is the best milk gargler in the fourth grade.

Today when everyone jumps up to run to the cafeteria, I hesitate. I walk to the door and tell Jasmine, "Go on without me today. I'm going to stay and talk to Lillian."

"You want me to stay with you?" Jasmine asks. "Lillian looks like she could use some friends."

"No, let's try one person at a time for now," I tell her. "My mom packed my lunch today, so I'm cool."

"Okay. I'll bring you one of those warm chocolate chip cookies if they have them."

"Bring a bunch of them!" I tell her with a grin.

Jasmine and the other students leave for the cafeteria. Lillian still has not left her seat. Miss Armstrong gives her a worried look.

"Can I stay here with Lillian?" I ask the teacher.

Miss Armstrong seems relieved. "What a great idea, Sassy," she says. "I'll run by the cafeteria and get you both some fruit."

"Teachers bring healthy stuff. Best friends bring chocolate chip cookies," I say, loud enough for Lillian to hear me. She gives me another small smile.

Miss Armstrong leaves and hurries down the hall. It's just me and Lillian. I walk back to my desk and plop down next to her. "Hi," I say. "My name is Sassy."

"That's a pretty name," Lillian whispers.

"I guess it's sorta scary starting a new school," I tell her.

"There's nothing worse," she replies.

"I've known the kids in my class since kindergarten. I'd hate to start over where I don't know anybody," I admit.

"This is my fourth school this year. Four schools for fourth grade. It's pretty awful."

"It must be hard to make friends," I say.

"I have no friends," she answers quietly.

"Yes, you do. You have at least one friend. Her name is Sassy!"

Lillian actually grins. "Is that your real name or a nickname?"

I tell her, "My name is Sassy Simone Sanford. It's not short for Sassafras or Sasquatch or something strange like that. It's just Sassy."

"Your name seems to fit you," Lillian says.

"Yeah, it's *so* me! My mom says she gave me that name right after I was born, when I stuck out my tongue at her."

Lillian giggles a little.

"I'm glad I didn't spit up or something gross like that when she first saw me. No telling what she would have called me! If I had laughed, I guess she might have called me Chuckles."

Lillian is almost giggling.

"And what if I had cried?" I say dramatically. "You might be talking to somebody named Sniffles or Booger!"

Lillian giggles some more. That makes me glad.

"So I guess Sassy isn't so bad. Actually, I really like it because it's just so me!"

I offer Lillian half of my chicken-and-cheese sandwich. Surprisingly, she takes it and nibbles a little of it.

"My mother is very proper," Lillian tells me. "She looked my name up in a book and found it means 'strong, beautiful flower' or something like that."

"I think it fits you," I tell her honestly.

"I'm not very strong," she admits. "Mom should have named me Petunia, which probably means 'scared to death at another new school'!"

We both laugh.

"I looked up my last name on the Internet, and I think Ling means 'sound of water flowing.'"

"Wow, how pretty."

"I guess. But mostly the water that seems to flow around me lately is just a bunch of tears."

"Where are you from?" I ask her as I finish my half of the sandwich.

"I'm from no place," she says, sadness in her voice.

"Well, where were you born?" I ask.

"Someplace in China is all that I know. My parents brought to me the United States when I was just a baby."

"I've never been out of the country — not even to Canada," I tell her.

"I've lived in ten different states and four different countries."

"Really? Can you speak any languages other than English?"

"Chinese. French. Spanish. A little German — we didn't stay in Germany very long."

I shake my head. "And I complain about my Spanish homework! You rock, Lillian."

This time she shakes her head. "As soon as I start feeling comfortable in one language, we have to leave. I've been to so many schools I've lost count."

"Bummer. What kind of jobs do your parents have? My dad is a science teacher and my mom sells insurance in a big office building downtown."

Lillian makes a face. "My dad and mom own a bunch of companies," she says. She does not sound very proud.

"That's a good thing, right?" I ask her.

"Good for them, I guess. It seems as though they like the people in their offices more than they like me." She sighs.

"What makes you say that?"

"They see their businesspeople every day. They travel all the time. They hardly ever see me." Lillian looks sad again.

"Who watches you while they travel?"

"I have a nanny."

"What's a nanny?" I ask her. I think that's a funny-sounding word.

"She is a very nice lady who makes sure I eat and reads to me at night. She takes care of me and keeps me safe. But she's not a mom."

I think about what it would be like if my mom was gone every day. I'd be messed up!

"I'm also friends with the butlers and maids and drivers," Lillian adds. "But they're not real family."

"So, are you rich?" I ask her. I am amazed because I've never met a real rich person before.

"I guess my parents are," Lillian answers slowly.

"Hey, I'm going to quit asking so many nosy questions," I say in a cheerful voice because Lillian is looking teary-eyed again.

I lift up my Sassy Sack, which is slung over the back of my desk chair. I dig down into it and pull out a small package of pink tissues and two juice boxes. I place one of them on her desk.

"That's a really awesome purse," Lillian says. She wipes her eyes with a tissue and sticks the straw into the juice box. "Mmm — fruit punch — my favorite."

I smile. "My grandmother gave it to me for my seventh birthday," I tell Lillian proudly. "She made it herself from treasures she had in her sewing kit."

"Cool!"

"She used pieces from a shimmery bridesmaid's dress, an old sequined prom dress, and this piece is lace from a tablecloth that came from Spain. It's got buttons and sparkles from old shoes and hats, along with pieces of earrings and necklaces and bracelets and stuff."

"My grandmother likes to sew also. And cook," Lillian tells me as she shyly touches my bag. "I don't get to see her very often."

"I understand. My grandmother lives in Florida in a big beach house, so we only get there during vacations. We were there during the last big hurricane! That was incredible!"

"That must have been scary," Lillian says.

"Yeah, for a minute," I tell her. I don't admit how really, really terrified I had been.

"I think the house I live in could stand up through a hurricane and a tornado. It's huge, like a castle," Lillian tells me. "But it's big and lonely most of the time."

"So, do you live close to the school?" I ask Lillian.

"I honestly don't know where it is — we just moved in last week. And my parents have already gone to another business meeting. They called me from London this morning before I left for school."

"Well, I'm glad they decided to send you to our school," I tell her with a smile.

"Me, too," Lillian admits quietly.

Miss Armstrong hurries back into the room carrying two apples, two oranges, and two bananas.

"See what I mean? Healthy stuff!" I whisper to Lillian.

We both laugh as Miss Armstrong places the fruit on our desks.

CHAPTER THREE

Experience and Explore

"**W**ell, I'm glad you two seem to be getting along," Miss Armstrong says, nodding with approval. "Has Sassy shown you her marvelous purple purse, Lillian? She calls it her Sassy Sack."

Lillian says, "It's the most awesome thing. I wish I had one like it."

Miss Armstrong chuckles. "It seems lots of the girls in her class admire it also."

I keep a million things in my Sassy Sack. Maybe two million. I've got stickers and hair stuff and jewelry and lotion and superglue and nail polish and lots of other things.

"What's your favorite color?" I ask Lillian.

"Pink," she replies with a smile.

"I coulda guessed that," I tell her. I reach down into my sack and pull out a small notebook. The cover is strawberry-colored and glittery. "Here's a welcome gift!" I say as I place it on her desk.

"For me? Thank you so much!" She picks it up and sniffs. "It's scented! It smells like fruit punch," she says with a grin.

"You're welcome. Now, *my* favorite color is purple. See?" Then I show her all my purple markers and pens and pencils. Many of them are covered with glitter or sparkles or feathers. "I also have purple bracelets and bangles, lavender necklaces, and violet hair clips. And lip gloss and eye shadow, which I'm not allowed to actually wear, and nail polish!"

"You're amazing!" she says.

We eat our fruit and finish our juice just as the bell rings for the end of lunch, and the rest of the class starts to come back in.

"I'll tell you a little about each kid as they come in the room," I whisper. "The boy with the big smile and the curly hair is Travis. He once got his head stuck in a chair."

Lillian laughs.

"Next to him are his friends Rusty and Ricky. They like to play practical jokes. Holly, the tall, slim girl behind them, is an awesome dancer. She wants to be a professional ballerina."

"Wouldn't that hurt your toes?" Lillian asks with a smile.

"I guess you're right. Coming in next are Basima, Iris, and Misty. They are all great singers. We had a big fourth-grade musical not too long ago, and they rocked the house!"

"I wish I could have seen it."

"But the best singer in the class, maybe even the whole school, is Carmelita. Her nickname is Caramel. That's Caramel talking to Princess. Princess is her real name, by the way."

"She looks a little like the kind of princess they put in picture books," Lillian says. Princess has long, flowing blonde hair. It ripples down her back like a golden stream.

"And the girl coming in last, carrying the warm cookies, is my best friend, Jasmine. I would say the girl in the blue-and-white uniform, but that's all of us!"

Jasmine comes over to us, gives me a cookie, and gives the other one to Lillian. I knew she would.

"I'll have my uniform tomorrow," Lillian says to both of us. "But it's nice wearing a pretty outfit for at least one day."

"My feelings exactly!" Jasmine says.

"Thanks for the cookie," Lillian says. "Everybody seems to be really nice here."

"Yep, we're all pretty cool," Jasmine tells her.

The bell rings and everybody is finally seated. I'm glad to see that Lillian looks a little more relaxed.

"You know, it's almost time for our fourth-grade creative experience projects," Miss Armstrong says as she begins the class.

She waits until the expected groans die down.

"When teachers use the words *creative* and *experience* in the same sentence, that usually means lots of work for us," Rusty whispers to Ricky.

Miss Armstrong ignores him. "First, you need to choose a topic. Remember, I don't want you to do a report — I want you to do a real exploration. You have to *experience* the information that you gather. When you finish, each of you will be an expert on that subject, and you can share it with the rest of us."

"Sounds like a report to me," Travis mumbles.

Miss Armstrong ignores Travis also. "Let me give you an example. Let's say you choose rocks as your area of investigation."

"All kinds of rocks?" Tandy asks.

"Good question, Tandy. You're already discovering that some topics are huge and you will need to concentrate on one small part. So maybe you just want to find out about rocks that are formed from volcanoes."

"Would building a volcano be a good idea to show what you have learned?" Princess asks.

"Excellent!" Miss Armstrong replies. She looks pleased,

like teachers do when they think we finally get what they're talking about.

"I just asked because my sister does a volcano every year for her science project, and we have about five of them in our garage."

Miss Armstrong shakes her head and chuckles. "Today I want each of you to try to find the area you want to investigate."

"Are we going to the library to do our research?" asks Princess.

"Eventually. Today I have a surprise for you," Miss Armstrong exclaims. "The new computer lab is finally up and running," she tells us, "and our class will be the first to use it."

"Sweet!" Ricky says.

"I know that most of you can run circles around me with your computer skills, but I manage to find what I need," Miss Armstrong confesses.

"I've had a computer since I was six years old," Travis boasts. "I'm an expert! If you get mixed up, Miss Armstrong, I'll show you what to do."

"Well, thank you, Travis, but I won't be teaching the computer class," she announces.

"Who's gonna teach it?" Misty asks.

"I am," says a tall, skinny man who strolls into the room at that moment. He wears blue jeans, a long-sleeved white shirt, a red leather vest, and bright red high-top sneakers. His hair is black and shaggy. He looks really young for a teacher.

"Nice shoes!" Rusty says with a whistle.

"Thanks! My name is Cecil Cannon, but you can call me Mr. C. I just graduated from the university, and I'm proud to say I'm a computer geek!"

Some of the kids giggle.

"I can take a computer apart and put all the little bitty pieces back together again. I know how to find files that get lost. I can upload and download and reload. I'm the man!"

"You gonna show us how to do all that stuff?" Rusty asks.

"And give up my super secrets? No way!" says Mr. C with a grin. "My job is to help you navigate the information superhighway. So leave your book bags here and walk with me down the hall to the new lab. Let's find some rockin' topics on these new supersonic computers! It's project time!"

As we get ready to leave, I grab my Sassy Sack and sling it over my shoulder.

"Oh, you won't need that, my dear," Mr. C says.

"Oh, yes, she will!" Jasmine and Holly say at the same time.

"Sassy takes that thing everywhere, Mr. C," Jasmine explains. "Stick around, and you'll see how useful it can be."

Mr. C says, "I was just trying to eliminate the need for purses. Miss Armstrong will be here in the classroom. But suit yourself. Don't let me be the one to separate a lady from her stuff!"

I smile at him. My Sassy Sack is more than a purse. It's like a part of me. Just touching it makes me feel happy.

I turn to Lillian and offer my hand to her. "Walk with me and Jasmine," I suggest. "And I'll finish telling you about the rest of the kids in our class while we're going to the lab."

Lillian looks grateful. As we head out the door, she whispers to me and Jasmine, "Can we stop by the bathroom on the way? It's been like *hours*!"

We crack up and head into the coolness of the main hall.

CHAPTER FOUR

Computers and Creations

The computer room even smells new. Most of our class-rooms have plain wooden or concrete floors, but this room has soft, dark blue carpet and light blue paint on the walls. The rows of computers look like a little techno-army dressed in new uniforms.

We take our seats. Everyone is hushed because the room is so impressive. Jasmine sits on one side of me. Lillian takes a seat on the other side.

Mr. C stands in front of the class and takes a deep breath. "Oh, boy, do I love this!" he says with real enthusiasm. "Brand-new equipment! I don't want to see anybody's pea-nut butter sandwich even close to these computers. No food or drinks in here — ever. Got it?"

"Gotcha, Mr. C," Rusty says. The rest of us nod our heads in agreement.

"Click the button on the left of your computers and let's give these babies a whirl!"

Clicks and soft whirs and beeps can be heard throughout the room. Everyone's computer lights up with a soft glow. The desktop appears on my screen, clear and ready to explore.

"Now, before we go to the Internet, I want to go over some basic stuff with you guys. I know many of you are very computer literate, but I want to make sure we are all on the same page."

Iris raises her hand. "We don't have a computer at home, so I might have a couple of extra questions. I've only used the one in the school library."

"Not a problem," Mr. C replies. "That's what I'm here for."

Princess asks then, "How will we save stuff we find?"

"You're getting ahead of me!" Mr. C says with a grin. "I would have prepared a PowerPoint lesson for you, but since they just hired me two days ago, we'll have to do it the old-fashioned way. I'll simply write it out for you today."

He walks over to the whiteboard.

"Looks like you'll be the first to write on it," Rusty says.

"I guess I'll have to use invisible ink!" Mr. C jokes. He looks in the cupboards and opens a few drawers. "Hmm, this is a trip. All this technology and they forgot to leave markers for the board!"

Travis and Rusty crack up.

Mr. C picks up the phone in the lab. "Let me contact the office and see if they can send some down here."

"You don't have to phone anybody, Mr. C," I call out.

"Why not, Sassy?" Mr. C asks me.

I pull my sack from the back of my chair, reach down into it, and pull out a handful of markers. "What color do you want?" I ask with a grin.

"Told you!" Jasmine and Holly say at the same time.

Mr. C scratches his head. "Thanks, Sassy," he says as he chooses a red marker and a green one. "You're a lifesaver!"

"I've got those, too!" I tell him. "All flavors."

Lillian and Jasmine are giggling.

Mr. C bows to me like I'm a queen or something, then goes back to the whiteboard to write the information.

In green marker he writes words like *monitor* and *keyboard* and *mouse*, and in red marker he lists things like *applications* and *search engine* and *browser*.

We all look at each other and frown.

Finally, Misty raises her hand.

"Yes," Mr. C says, stopping his colorful writing for a minute.

Misty tells him, "Uh, I don't have a computer at home, either, but all of us know this stuff already. Lots of us have apps and browsers on our cell phones. Every day we play video games and share stuff with each other through the Internet. The stuff you are writing on the board we learned in first grade."

Mr. C looks at us, then cracks up. "You know, you're right! You guys could probably teach me! Click on the Internet icon on your screen, find your search engine, and type in what you want to explore. Go for it!"

We all kinda sigh with relief and get started. Keyboards click and computers hum. Mr. C walks around and answers questions if anybody has them. Nobody needs the vocabulary words he listed.

"What are you going to do your project on?" Jasmine asks Holly, who is sitting on the other side of her.

"Dance, of course!" Holly replies. "I think I want to find out more about lyrical ballet. It's a little different from the strict European style that my teacher uses."

"Sounds like it will be fun to explore," Jasmine replies.

"Oh, yes," Holly says with excitement in her voice. "And for my demonstration to the class, I'll perform a lyrical ballet!"

"Nice."

"What about you, Jasmine?" I ask. "Are you going to do some kind of performance, too?"

"No way," Jasmine replies while she's typing. "I started

with my name, and I decided to explore all sweet-smelling flowers."

"What a great idea," I tell her.

"And you know what? Many of the flowers that smell good have cool-sounding names. Like gardenia. And magnolia. They're fun to say."

"Gar-dee-nia!" I say real slow. "You're right!"

"But my favorite is bougainvillea," Jasmine tells me. "Boo-gan-veel-lee-ah! Boo-gan-veel-lee-ah! I could say it all day."

"Sounds like booger!" Travis hollers from two seats down.

Jasmine just rolls her eyes at him and gets back to work.

Mr. C stops by my seat and returns my markers. "Thanks, Sassy. They tell me you carry just about everything in that purse of yours."

"Pretty much," I tell him. "I always seem to have just what's needed. I like to feel useful."

"Have you decided on a topic yet?" Mr. C asks.

"Not quite. Still looking," I say. "I'm getting close, though."

He moves on to another student, but I still have no idea at all what to do.

So I ask Lillian, who is sitting next to me, "What are you looking up for your project?"

She sighs. "I hope I'm here long enough to complete it. But I've always been interested in whales," she replies.

"Whales?" I gasp. That's the last thing I would have expected this tiny girl to say.

"It started when we were living in San Francisco, by the ocean."

"You're gonna bring a whale to class for your demonstration?" I ask with a smile.

"No, silly. Did you know that you can adopt a baby whale or dolphin to help save them from extinction? There are all kinds of websites about how to save ocean animals."

"Yeah, I know. Our family once helped save a nest of sea turtles," I tell her. "That made me feel real good."

"See, you get it. Maybe I'll look into whale songs as part of my project. They make music, you know."

"Really?"

"Their songs sound really sad sometimes," Lillian says. "Sad and lonely, just like me." She returned to her computer screen, suddenly very quiet again.

I glance at the mysterious girl in pink. Dozens of questions bounce in my head, but I can't ask any of them. I wish I could help her be happy.

I search a few ideas for this project, but nothing sounds very interesting to me. I look up *makeup* and *cosmetics*, especially the glittery kind. But my mom doesn't let me wear makeup anyway, so that would be useless.

I look up *sewing* and *making purses*, but that seems hard. Grammy made my sack and one for herself, but I don't think I want to try it.

I daydream for a minute, thinking of Grammy. I remember the time she visited and we all went out to dinner at a fancy restaurant. That had been glorious — until all of us got stuck in an elevator!

But the food had been *so* good that night.

I wish I could cook like that. Elegant and glamorous. A fancy feast.

Then, suddenly, I know what I want to do! I have discovered the perfect idea. I can have fun and maybe put a smile on Lillian's face at the same time.

Jasmine asks me then, "So what are *you* exploring for your project, Sassy? Sparkles? Glitter gloss? Purple purses?"

I grin at her and shake my head. "None of that. I'm going to learn to cook!"

"Cook?"

"Yes. And then I'm going to give a splendid and swanky dinner party!"

"How are you going to do that?"

"I have no idea. I still have to figure that part out!" I tell her with a grin.

CHAPTER FIVE

Dreaming of a Dinner Party

We visit the computer lab every day after lunch now. Mr. C asks questions, offers suggestions, and cracks really lame computer jokes.

"Why did the computer sneeze?" he asks.

"It had a virus," Travis answers quickly.

"What do you call a computer superhero?" Mr C asks next.

"A screen saver!" Misty replies.

"You guys are swift!" Mr. C says. "Here's one you don't know. What do you get if you cross a computer with an elephant?"

Nobody calls out an answer.

"Gotcha!" he says with glee. "You get lots and lots of memory!"

We all groan, but he makes the class fun, and he really does know lots of tricks and shortcuts to help us find information for our research.

Mr. C gives each of us a flash drive to keep all the material we collect for our projects. My drive is full of recipes and menus and place settings. There's so much I don't know. When my mom cooks a meal, I wait for her to fix it, then I sit down and eat. I just know it tastes good when she puts it on my plate. I don't pay much attention to what she's doing. But I'm starting to watch her more.

Mr. C stops by my computer and scans the material I have on the screen. "I think your project is absolutely the yummiest!" he declares. "When are you going to have this big party?"

"I'm not sure. I haven't asked my mom yet," I admit.

"Sounds like your next big step," he replies. "Hard to have a dinner party in the school parking lot!"

"My mom is cool, and my family will help. My older brother, Sabin, might eat up all the food, though!"

"That's what brothers are for," Mr. C says with a laugh. "Especially if you serve anything sweet."

"You've met my brother!" I joke.

Mr. C laughs again. "Take your flash drive home and show your mom all the wonderful research you've done. Tomorrow you should think about recipes and a shopping list."

"Shopping?"

"Sure. Do you have all the ingredients for the recipes you want to prepare?"

"I haven't really thought about it."

He gives me one of those knowing "teacher" smiles. I start typing a list of food I will need. It's a long list.

Mr. C moves on to Lillian's computer.

Lillian now wears a blue-and-white uniform like everybody else. But I will always remember her as the tiny new girl dressed all in pink. She's still very quiet, but she is starting to make friends. However, each morning she arrives in the limousine and leaves every afternoon when the driver comes to pick her up. We still know very little about her.

"How's your project coming?" Mr. C asks her.

"I've downloaded whale songs and dolphin songs. I've got tons of pictures of whales and dolphins — sharks, too."

"Do sharks sing?"

"I don't think so," Lillian replies with a soft giggle. "I just like them because they are so fierce. They are the exact opposite of the gentle dolphin."

Mr. C nods with approval. "What will you do next?"

"I think I'm going to make a movie using clips from the photos and videos I've found," Lillian answers.

"Great idea! With music?" Mr. C asks.

"Oh, yes. I want to do two sound tracks. One with whale songs and one with real music — like maybe the theme song from that movie *Free Willy*."

"Wonderful film."

"I've seen it forty-seven times," Lillian admits. "For a long time it was the only one I had on DVD."

Mr. C cracks up. "You truly *are* an expert!"

"Only on whales," she says. "Every time we moved, I'd watch it on a little DVD player in the back of the limo. Willy the whale was my friend for a while, sort of."

"Well, I hope you get to stay and make real friends here," Mr. C said. "I've heard that whales don't make very good pets. They poop in the bathtub!"

Lillian laughs and asks him, "Can you show me how to make two sound tracks work together?"

Mr. C pulls up a chair and shows Lillian what to do.

Jasmine, sitting on the other side of me, is still checking out websites on flowers. I keep typing and searching and planning my party.

I whisper to Jasmine, "Will you come to my dinner party?"

"You know it!" she replies. "When is it?"

"I don't know. I haven't asked Mom yet."

"Better get to it!"

"I will. Tonight. Who else should I invite?" I ask her.

"All the girls in our class," Jasmine answers.

"What about the boys?"

Jasmine looks around the room. "Sure, why not? They might feel bad if you leave them out."

"That's a lot of people," I say. "You think my mom will put up with a whole bunch of fourth graders in her house?"

"Your mom puts up with Sabin and that crazy dog of his. She can handle a few kids," Jasmine replies.

"How do I know how many people are coming?" I ask her. I've never thought about stuff like this.

"Give everybody an invitation," Jasmine says. "And ask them to tell you if they are coming. That's called an RSVP."

"Invitations! Brilliant!"

"Duh!" she says. She goes back to her flower research.

I turn back to my computer and look up *party invitations*. There's probably a million websites listed. I just want something easy I can design myself and print out for my friends. It takes me about fifteen minutes, but I find something I like. I save it on my flash drive just as the bell rings for the end of class.

I toss the flash drive into my Sassy Sack, sling it over my shoulder, and leave the room with my friends.

At the end of the day, Jasmine and I get on the dirty yellow school bus with lots of other kids. Lillian quietly steps into her limousine and is whisked away by her driver. That limo looks freshly waxed every day. Even on rainy days it shines.

CHAPTER SIX

Lima Beans and a Boom Box

"**H**ow was school, Sassy?" Mom asks as I walk into the kitchen.

I have changed into purple jeans and a yellow T-shirt decorated with silver sparkles. I feel great because this is *so* not like my uniform!

"Great. What's for dinner?" I ask her. "It smells good in here."

She looks pleased. "That's the pineapple upside-down cake you smell, Sassy. But we're also having baked chicken and lima beans and those yummy pan-fried potatoes you like. And salad, of course."

"Can I skip the lima beans?" I ask her with a grin.

"You usually do," she says, then sighs. "Your sister will eat only veggies. Your brother will eat anything on his plate. You're just my picky eater."

Mom loves to cook, and we love to eat what she fixes.

Mostly. We don't eat a lot of fast food in our house. It's a special treat when Mom lets us order pizza or get burgers and fries.

The oven bell dings. "You want to take the cake out of the oven for me?" she asks. "Put on those big mitts and very carefully take it out and place it on the counter."

I pull on the giant mitts. They go all the way up my arms. When I open the oven, the hot air feels good on my face. The warm smell of soft, sugary pineapple surrounds me. I carefully take the pan from the rack and place it on the counter. I close the oven door.

"Great job, Sassy!" Mom says.

"I can cook, too," I tell her.

"I know that," she says. "I'm not ready for you to use the oven by yourself, but I've seen you make hot dogs and sandwiches."

"I can make bologna bowls in the microwave!" I remind her proudly.

"Our own secret family recipe!" Mom says with a smile.

I think Sabin invented bologna bowls when he was about my age. It's the easiest recipe in the world. You slap a piece of bologna on a microwavable plate and rip a slice of cheese into pieces. The cheese goes into the center of the bologna. You put the whole thing into the microwave for twenty seconds. The bologna curls into a bowl around the melted cheese. Yummy instant meal!

"Uh, I'd like to do more, Mom," I begin. "I want to plan a dinner party."

"Really? What brought this on?"

"Well, it's sort of a school project. We have to research a subject, then do a demonstration of what we've learned."

"Your teacher is requiring you to prepare a dinner?" Mom looks confused.

"No, Mom," I say patiently. "We get to pick any subject we want. Jasmine chose flowers. Holly decided to do her project on dance."

"And you chose food? Sounds like a project Sabin would do."

"No, my project is not just about *eating* food. It's about meals and recipes and table settings and decorations! I want to do something really special. I want it to be dazzling!"

"Hmm. A dazzling dinner party," Mom says as she stirs the potatoes in the pan. "That sounds like you, Sassy. Let me hear more about this grand idea of yours."

I tell her with excitement, "I want to send special invitations to all my friends. Something sparkly and purple, of course."

"Of course."

"And I have recipes I want to fix. All by myself. I can show you all the cool stuff I found online."

"I'm not sure if I want you loose in my kitchen, Sassy. Ovens are hot, and burners — well, they can burn you."

"I figured you'd say that. Nothing I'm fixing requires the stove. And only a couple of things need the microwave. I can cook everything myself."

Sabin strolls into the kitchen, a long string of red licorice hanging from his mouth. His dog, Zero, trots behind him. "What are *you* gonna cook, Little Sister?" He sucks in the rest of the candy with a whoosh and a smack.

"Don't call me little! And I'm going to cook a whole meal for all my friends!"

Sabin is twelve, skinny as a pencil, and I think he lives on nothing but sweets. Chocolate, peppermint, caramel. He gobbles candy all day long.

"You can hardly see over the top of the stove," he teases.

"I'm big enough," I insist. "If you're nice to me, I'll let you taste some of my creations."

He pulls another piece of licorice from his jeans pocket and hands it to me. It's covered with lint. "Want some?" he offers.

"I'm going to let you keep that," I tell him with a laugh. But I might use some red string licorice for one of my recipes.

"You're gonna let her do this, Mom?" Sabin asks. He tosses a doggie treat to Zero.

"We'll see," she replies. That's the answer that moms always give while they are still deciding on things their kids want to do.

"Yum, pineapple upside-down cake!" my sixteen-year-old sister, Sadora, says. She smells like peach lotion as she waltzes into the kitchen. She picks up the top from one of the pots on the stove. "And lima beans! I love limas!"

Sabin and I roll our eyes at each other. Who eats lima beans on purpose?

Sadora is really pretty. Of course I'd never tell her that. Even though she's always buying makeup with her friends when they go to the mall, she really doesn't need it. She could be a model like the girls I see in teen magazines.

"Sassy wants to give a dinner party!" Sabin tells her.

"Really? That's cool, Sassy," Sadora tells me as she puts forks and spoons and knives on the table. "What's the occasion? There's no holiday coming soon."

"Well, it started out as a school research project. I got to thinking about that elegant dinner we had with Grammy. . . ."

"Don't remind me!" Sabin says with a laugh. "That's when I had to go to the bathroom *so* bad, and we were stuck in a stupid elevator!" He puts the plates and napkins on the table.

All of us crack up. "Anyway, I decided I want to fix a really special meal and then invite my friends to eat it!"

"What will you cook?" Sadora asks.

"Mom won't let me use the oven, so my recipes don't need it."

"How are you going to cook without cooking?" Sabin asks. "You're gonna serve hard macaroni pieces and raw chicken?" He looks doubtful.

"You'll see," I tell him.

"Do you want me to help?" Sadora asks.

"I want to do the cooking all by myself," I tell her. "I can do this. Really, I can."

"This I gotta see," Sabin says. Before he puts the glasses on the table, he pours milk into a huge one and gulps it down.

I tell Sadora, "But if you could take pictures of the dinner party, I'll have something to put into my project presentation at school."

"Great idea! I'm taking a photography class at school, you know."

Daddy comes into the kitchen carrying an old-fashioned boom box. He is scratching his head.

"I can't get this thing to work," he says, complaining. "I wanted to play some music for us while we eat."

"Let me run outside and see if I can find a caveman to fix it!" Sabin teases.

Daddy sits down at the table, still pushing buttons and shaking the dusty old machine. "Dinner smells great, Susan," he says. "Love those pan-fried potatoes! But my box seems to be busted."

"Why don't you put your music on an iPod like the rest of the world, Daddy?" Sadora asks him.

"Yeah, Dad, you're a science teacher. You should have the very latest in technology for your students, and you should give your son an iPod, too!" Sabin says with a grin.

"It's not that I don't like the new stuff — it's just I've had this box for so long and it plays all my old CDs. It's old and mellow like I am."

"Did you plug it in?" I ask. I don't see a cord.

Daddy makes a face at Sabin. "Zero chewed the cord to pieces!" Daddy replies.

"My bad," Sabin says, slumping down in his seat. The dog has sense enough to hide under the table.

"Maybe it's the batteries," Daddy says. He pulls out four huge D cells and they clatter onto the table.

"Can't we do this after dinner, Sam?" Mom says in a weary voice.

"This will just take a minute, sweetie," he replies.

Mom makes a face, then opens the kitchen drawer. She pulls out four C-size batteries and gives them to him.

"These are the wrong size!" Daddy complains.

I'm hungry, and I have an idea. I reach for my sack. My change purse hangs from it by a key chain. The change purse is purple and the name *Sassy* is written on it in sparkly letters. I count out twelve quarters and give them to Daddy.

"Is this to buy new batteries?" he asks.

"Try this, Daddy," I suggest. "Put three quarters in each slot with a C battery."

Our whole family looks at me in amazement.

Daddy fiddles with the batteries and quarters for a moment, clicks the back of the machine shut, and pushes a button on the front.

Like magic, lovely classical music floats out of the ancient speakers.

"Thanks, Sassy!" Daddy says. "I wish I'd thought of that!"

"Yeah, thanks," Sabin agrees. "One more minute and I was gonna have to put some gravy on a battery and eat it!"

The music really is a nice touch as we eat.

Dinner is yummy.

Except for the lima beans.

CHAPTER SEVEN
Creating Invitations

After dinner, I tell Sabin and Sadora that I'll help Mom with the dishes. They bolt out of the kitchen before I have a chance to change my mind.

As I stack the plates in the dishwasher, Mom says, "Cleanup after a dinner party is huge, Sassy. You won't believe the mess!"

"I promise to clean up," I tell her.

"Actually, that's the end of the list. Let's start at the beginning. Who are you inviting?"

I hesitate a little. "Uh, everybody in Miss Armstrong's class."

"Good grief, Sassy! That's a zillion people!"

"Well, I can't invite some and not others. I don't want to hurt anyone's feelings."

"How many kids are in your class?"

"Less than a zillion!" I tell her with a grin. "I think we have about twenty-five."

"That's still an awful lot of nine- and ten-year-olds running around my house," Mom says, shaking her head.

"Not all of them will come," I say quickly. I have no idea if that's true, but it sounds good.

"And what happens when they get here? What will they do and what will they eat?"

"I've been thinking about that," I reply. "I'm going to prepare some food ahead of time. The rest I'm going to let the kids make. When everybody is finished making their recipes —"

"You mean when everybody is finished making a mess!" Mom interrupts me with a smile.

"Then we eat."

She sits down at the table and runs her hands through her hair. "This isn't going to be easy, Sassy."

"Please, Mom." I give her my very best sweet smile.

She shakes her head. I know she's giving in. "So what will you serve at this extravaganza?"

"Oh, I like that word!" I tell her. I reach into my sack, which is hanging on the back of my chair. I pull out a pink notebook and open it. "Here are my recipes," I tell her proudly.

Mom looks at what I have written. My printing is very neat. I write in purple ink whenever I can.

"I'm impressed," Mom says. "You have some great ideas here."

"I used pieces of recipes I found online, but most of them I made up myself!" I tell her with excitement.

"Like the Purple Passion Milk Shake?" Mom chuckles.

"Ice cream and grape juice, mostly," I explain. "That one needs a blender. Or a very strong person to shake the jar."

"I see you have lots of dishes made with fruit," Mom says with approval.

"Most everything I'm preparing is full of healthy stuff," I tell her proudly.

"Sprinkled with sugar whenever possible," Mom adds.

"Well, yeah!" I turn a page in my notebook and show her the shopping list on the page I printed out on the computer, which I taped inside. "My teacher suggested I figure out what I would need to buy to make this happen."

"Whoa!" Mom says. "This is huge! That's a whole shopping cart!"

I smile the sweet "Please, Mom" smile once more.

She shakes her head, but I know she's going to say yes. "When do you want to have this dazzling dinner party?" Mom asks.

"A week from Saturday?" I say with a question mark in my voice. "That gives us ten days to get ready."

"What about your invitations?"

"Ooh, let me show you!" I pull the flash drive from my sack, and we head for the computer in the family room.

Just as I plug the drive into the machine, Sabin complains, "I was just getting ready to play *Space Blasters*, Little Sister."

"You're watching television," I reply.

"I can do both," he tells me.

"Not this time!"

I click on the icon, find the file, and my invitation pops up on the screen.

"Awesome, Sassy," my sister says as she looks over my shoulder. "Who designed that?"

"I did!" I tell her with pride.

The invitation is done in a purple font. It's just a piece of typing paper folded in half, but I've got pictures of fireworks and sparklers decorating the front. I also have photos of lit dinner candles and a fancy table setting with real china and silverware.

The front of it reads, in fancy lettering, You Are Invited to a Dazzling Dinner Party!

Inside it says,

I'm giving a special Sassy feast.
Yummy food. Everything a different color!
You get to cook some of it!

You get to eat all of it!
Come hungry!

Then I give the date and the time and my address and phone number.

"Can I print it out, Mom?"

Mom is starting to look as excited as I am. She opens a desk drawer and pulls out a ream of lavender computer paper. "I've been saving this for a special Sassy occasion," she says.

"Awesome! Thanks, Mom." I load the printer and print out one page as a test.

"I think you messed up, Little Sister," Sadora says.

"Huh?"

She takes the paper from me and folds it in half. The front is upside down, and what is supposed to be on the inside is on the outside.

"What do I do?" It looked okay on the screen. I don't know how to fix it.

Sadora scoots into the chair, pushing me out. She clicks a couple of keys, hits SAVE, then pushes PRINT once more.

This time the invitation comes out just right. "I'm the queen of the machine!" she says, standing and taking a bow.

I print out thirty invitations — a few extra just in case.

"What next?" Sadora asks.

"I'm going to use purple and pink glitter glue to make the

invitations sparkle, then I'll give them out at school tomorrow." I'm already digging for the glitter in my sack.

"I think you forgot something, Sassy," Mom says.

I look at the invitation carefully. "What?" I ask.

"Your RSVP. How will you know how many kids are coming?"

"Oops!"

I sit back down at the computer. I find the fancy font I used, click to purple ink once more, and type in **Please tell me if you are coming.**

Under that I type **Your Name** and **Your Phone Number.**

I include two lines long enough for them to write on. Then I put two large squares with the words **Yes** and **No** printed under each one.

I add one more sentence: **Please return this to me by Friday.** (Because my mom is taking me shopping on Saturday.)

"Great job, Sassy," Mom says. She hands it back to me.

"Stick that inside each invitation," Sadora suggests.

I carefully print out thirty of the RSVP sheets, then head to the kitchen table to decorate everything.

"What do you think?" I ask Sadora. She sits down and decorates an invitation without me even asking.

"You have glitter on your nose," she says with a laugh. "And I think you're going to have a glorious, glamorous dinner."

CHAPTER EIGHT

A Surprise from the Sassy Sack

When Mom drops me off at school the next morning, I am shivering with excitement.

"Wait till you see what I have in my Sassy Sack," I whisper to Holly and Carmelita. We are waiting on the front steps for the bell to ring.

"Another musical instrument?" Holly asks.

I play the piccolo, which is just small enough to fit into my sack. "No," I tell her with a smile. "Not this time."

"A video game?" Carmelita guesses.

"Not even close."

I see Jasmine hopping out of her mom's car. She runs to join us. "Did you bring them?" she asks. She and I had talked on the phone just before I went to bed.

"Yep!" I say, clutching my bag close to my chest.

"What is it you've got hidden in your sack today, Sassy?" Travis asks.

"A surprise for everybody," I tell him.

"Food?" he asks hopefully.

"Candy?" Rusty adds.

"Not exactly," I say. "And not yet."

"You're not making any sense," Travis replies.

"I know!" I agree.

All of the girls laugh.

Just then the shiny black limousine snakes into the driveway. "Here comes Lillian!" announces Rusty.

The driver walks to her door like he does every day. Lillian steps out and looks around. She always looks a little scared when she first gets out of the car. Like maybe we won't be there waiting. Then she spots us.

We wave.

Travis shouts, "Hey, Lillian!"

She gives us all a huge smile, waves, and hurries to where we stand. She looks really happy to see us.

The driver whooshes away.

We no longer ask about where she lives or if she's rich. We don't care. She's just Lillian, and we're glad she's here.

"Hi, Lillian," Jasmine says. "Where'd you get that awesome blue-and-white outfit?"

"Oh, yes, I wish I had one just like it!" I add.

Lillian giggles.

"Wait! I *do* have one just like it!" Holly says, joining in.

"Oh, no! We all do!" I grab my neck like I'm choking. "Somebody has dressed us all in uniforms! *Ack!*"

We are still laughing as the bell rings and we march into the school.

When I get to Miss Armstrong's class, I walk up to her desk.

"Good morning, Sassy Simone," she says in her musical-sounding voice.

"Hi, Miss Armstrong. Um, I have something I need to pass out to the class. It's about my project."

"Let me see what you have, dear," she says kindly.

"Well, I decided to give a dinner party for my project, and I need to invite my guests."

"You didn't leave anyone out, did you?"

"No, I have an invitation for every kid in the class," I tell her. "There's even one for you and Mr. C." I pause. "But you don't really have to come."

She smiles at that.

I reach down into my sack and pull out the invitations. Mom said to place them in a plastic bag so I wouldn't get glitter all over my sack. But glitter is never a bad thing.

The purple sheets are a little heavy and a couple are stuck together. "I guess I got carried away with shiny glue!" I tell the teacher.

Miss Armstrong looks at them and nods her head with

approval. "Lovely, Sassy," she says. Then she says to the class, "Sassy has something to give everyone before we begin."

"My project is a party," I explain. "And I want you all to come."

"So that's where the food will be," Travis says as I give him his invitation.

"More food than you can eat, Travis," I tell him. "And lots and lots of sweet stuff."

"I'm there!" he says.

I give every student a shiny, sticky, glittery invitation. I feel very proud. Everyone is admiring how cool they look.

"Inside each one is a sheet that tells me if you can come or not. That way I know how much stuff to buy. I need that back as soon as you ask your parents."

"You sound like a teacher," Rusty says.

"I hope not!" I tell him with a grin.

"What should we wear?" Jasmine asks.

"Who cares?" Travis yells out.

"We do!" Holly and Jasmine and Misty answer at the same time.

I think it's a great question. "No uniforms!" I announce loudly.

Everybody cheers.

"It's sorta fancy, but you'll be cooking part of the time, so just wear something comfortable," I explain. "I'm wearing something with sparkles!"

"I think we already knew that," Jasmine says.

"We'll be cooking? What do you mean?" Carmelita asks.

"That is going to be the fun part!" I reply with excitement. "We won't be cooking on the stove, but you'll get to make your own fancy sandwiches. The bread and the meat are cut into designs with cookie cutters! Or you'll get to dip bananas into melted chocolate."

"Now that sounds like *my* kind of assignment," Travis says.

Miss Armstrong stands up then and says, "Okay, enough of this for now. Speaking of assignments, let's get started with class. I know everybody is looking forward to Sassy's dazzling dinner party, but it's time for math."

We all groan and dig for our math books and papers. Every time we go next door for math class, I think time stops. It is the longest hour in the day.

As we are walking to math, I ask Lillian, "Do you think you will be able to come to my dinner party?"

"I'm not sure. I hope I can," she replies quietly.

"Uh, would it help if my mom called your mom?"

She shakes her head. "No, that's not a good idea. I'll talk to her when she returns."

"She's out of town?"

"Most of the time," Lillian says. I can hear sadness in her voice.

"What about your dad?"

Lillian rarely talks about her family, so we take our time as we head down the hall.

"I hardly ever see my folks since they travel so much for business," she says softly.

I put my arm around her. Her shoulders are tinier than mine! I give her a quick squeeze as we walk into the room.

"Don't you think Mr. Olsen's head looks like a lightbulb?" I whisper. I'm trying to make her smile.

Lillian's giggle always sounds like wind chimes tinkling.

Our math teacher, Mr. Olsen, is completely bald. His head shines under the classroom lights.

"Not those new curly energy-saver bulbs," she whispers back.

We both laugh really hard then.

Mr. Olsen is a good teacher, but I have trouble paying attention. Even though he has no hair on his head, he has fuzzy brown hair growing out of his nose and ears. I try to concentrate on numbers, but I keep watching his nose hair wiggle as he talks.

Jasmine gobbles numbers like slippery noodles. Numbers come to me more like lumpy mashed potatoes. It's so not fair.

Mr. Olsen begins, "Today I will try to show you that math is necessary to our everyday lives. Even the lives of kids."

Travis raises his hand. "Can't I just use my calculator?"

"Suppose it breaks or you lose it?"

"I'll use my fingers!"

"And take off your shoes and socks if the number is bigger than ten?"

"Stinky!" Rusty says. "Please don't!"

"So, Sassy," Mr. Olsen says. "If Lucy buys twenty strawberries for five dollars, how much does each berry cost?"

Why does he start with me? "Huh?" I say. "Who's Lucy?"

Some of the kids giggle.

"We're talking about shopping today," he explains patiently.

"Oh. I'm sorry. What was the question?"

Jasmine raises her hand. "Each strawberry costs twenty-five cents."

Jasmine always knows the right answer. That's okay with me.

Mr. Olsen turns to the class again. "Now here's another question. There is a video game I want to buy. The original price was forty dollars. It's been marked down fifteen percent. How much does it cost now?"

Several kids raise their hands with the answer.

Mr. Olsen calls on Lillian. "Thirty-four dollars," she says. Lillian likes math. So do Travis and Princess. Jasmine probably dreams about math problems. Me, I just hope I don't have to take off my shoes and socks.

I survive math, and I even answer one question right. Mr. Olsen looks pleased. The bell rings and we rush to lunch.

Lillian sits with us at lunch now. We squeeze together on the bench at the fourth-grade table. Everybody wants to talk about my dinner party.

"So, what's for dinner, Sassy?"

"Fried chicken?" Travis asks. "That's my favorite!"

"Nothing fried at all," I explain. "My mom would have a heart attack if I tried to stand in front of the stove and stir hot grease in a pan!"

"Then let your mom fry the chicken," Ricky says as he takes a big bite of his cookie.

I try to explain. "You don't get it. It's my party, so I'm cooking."

"I bet it's just peanut butter sandwiches," Ricky says as he gobbles a French fry.

I grab one of his fries. "No way. I'm serving elegant food!"

"You know how to cook?" Princess asks.

"Yep! At least well enough to fix what we are having."

"Can you give us a hint?" asks Holly.

"Okay. Everything I serve will be a different color. Like bubble-gum pink and bubble-gum blue soda."

"Sweet!"

"And green pudding."

"Yuck!"

"And orange cream pie!"

"Now you're talking!"

"Do you know how to make dirt pudding?" Travis asks.

"Now who's talking about yucky?" Jasmine says.

"We learned how to do it in Cub Scouts a couple of years ago," Travis explains. "Maybe I'll bring some so you guys can taste it."

"Cool! Thanks," I say.

"Do you want us to bring anything?" Carmelita asks.

"Not really," I tell her. "But it's nice of you to ask."

Lillian is usually quiet at lunch. She just listens to our silly conversations like she's breathing in warm summer air. But just before lunch is over she says, "I think your project is the nicest of all. It's more than a report — it's a party! It's awesome you have included your friends. And me."

"Well, I sure hope you can come!" I tell her. "I want ALL my friends to be there."

"Me, too." She sips on a juice box. "Me, too."

CHAPTER NINE

Zooming with a Shopping Cart

"**H**urry up, Mom!" I cry out impatiently.

It's finally Saturday, and we are going shopping for the ingredients for my party. I have already eaten a bowl of cereal for my breakfast.

"I can't believe you're up so early on a Saturday morning," Mom says. She is cutting out coupons at the kitchen table.

"This is important!" I tell her.

She glances around the table. It is full of newspapers and clippings and magazine ads. "Now, where did I put that envelope? I can't just take a stack of coupons in my hands."

I reach down into my sack, dig around for a moment, then pull out a small plastic sandwich bag. "Will this work?" I ask.

Mom smiles. "You always have just what I need, Sassy." She puts the coupons into the bag, snaps it closed, and tosses it into her purse. Her bag is ordinary looking. It's dusty brown fake leather, and she's had it, like, a million years.

My bag, however, is unique!

"Sabin and Sadora are still asleep," I tell her.

"It's Saturday morning! I expect they'll just be getting up when we get back."

"I called Jasmine and she said she's waiting on her front porch," I tell Mom as we head to the car.

"Two giggly girls out to spend all my money!" Mom shakes her head.

The car backs out of the driveway. I roll down my window and let the cool air hit my face. I love the morning. It's the best part of the day.

"Thanks for letting me have this party, Mom," I tell her softly. "I feel so grown-up."

She smiles as she turns the corner. I think she likes mornings, too. "How many kids are coming?" she asks.

"Well, I passed out twenty-five invitations. Fourteen kids gave me their RSVP pages and said they could come. A couple of kids will be out of town, some have other stuff to do next Saturday, and Miss Armstrong and Mr. C both had other plans."

"Hmm. Fourteen. Plus you and your sister and brother. I guess we can handle that." She turns onto Jasmine's street.

"I hope it's fifteen," I tell her.

"How come?"

"There is a new girl in our class named Lillian."

"Yes, you've told me about her. The girl in the limo."

"She is the only one who has not answered. And I *really* want her to come."

"Well, maybe she'll let you know on Monday. I'd like to meet her."

We pull into Jasmine's driveway, and she is already yelling into her house to tell her mom she's gone. She runs to the car and hops in the backseat. I move to the back to sit with her.

"This is so cool!" Jasmine says as we snap on our seat belts. "Hi, Mrs. Sanford."

"Good morning, Jasmine. We can't get you girls up for school, but for a Saturday shopping trip you're awake before the birds!"

"Duh!" I say. "Shopping beats sleeping any day! Even at a grocery store."

"How many boys are coming to the party?" Jasmine asks me.

"Five. Travis, Rusty, Ricky, Charles, and Abdul."

"Boys eat a lot," Jasmine comments.

"Tell me about it. My brother, Sabin, can eat a whole box of Frosted Flakes in one sitting. And then he still says he's hungry!"

Jasmine laughs. "What about the girls?"

I pull a notebook from my sack and check my list. "Let's see. Carmelita and Misty. Iris, Princess, Basima, and Josephina. Holly, Tandy, and you. That's nine girls, so far, not counting me."

"What about Lillian?"

"When I saw her at school yesterday, she said she was still trying to get permission. She looked really sad when she got in her limo after school."

"What's up with that?" Jasmine wondered. "If she *is* rich, it seems like she'd be happy, right?"

"I used to think if I had like a zillion dollars, I'd be *too* happy. But now I think maybe not," I tell Jasmine.

"Well, I really hope she can come," Jasmine says.

"Me, too."

We pull into the supermarket lot, jump out, and grab a cart.

"Wait!" I say, just as Mom is locking the car door. "We forgot the reusable grocery bags!"

"Thanks, Sassy," Mom says. "I always leave those things in the car. I remember that I have them when I get to the checkout!"

I grab the bags from the trunk and throw them into the cart.

But before we move even an inch, we hear *Squeak! Thunk! Squeak! Thunk!*

"What's up with this?" Jasmine asks.

"We found a shopping cart with issues!" I tell her with a laugh.

"Here's another one," she says as she gets a new cart. This one rolls smoothly.

"Much better!" Mom says with relief.

"I'll push!" Jasmine says with glee.

We head for the sliding glass door.

"And I'll grab what's on my list!" I tell Mom.

"And I get to pay?" Mom replies with a smile.

"I'll give you all the allowance money I've saved up," I offer sweetly.

"And how much is that?" she asks.

"Almost eleven dollars!"

"Well, I can just retire and go live on an island!" she tells me with a laugh.

The store is brightly lit and faint music plays in the background. If I squint my eyes, the color I see most is red. Red potato chip packages just as we walk in. Red candy wrappers on the left. They look so good I want to toss them in our cart.

But I pull my list from my sack. I printed it out at school.

I know exactly what we need. "Let's go to the fruit and vegetable aisle first!" I say.

Jasmine zooms the cart in that direction. Mom follows behind us. I can't believe how cool she is about all this.

"Look at all this stuff!" Jasmine cries. "Somebody must stay up all night long stacking tomatoes in pretty little mountains."

"Tomatoes are on my list," I say.

"Ooh, yuck!" Jasmine points to a rotten, squashed tomato right on top of the pile. "Red juice is oozing out!"

I touch it and more juice erupts from it. We crack up.

"Okay, girls," Mom says. "Grab a couple of onions from that pile over there. And get five firm tomatoes. We'll leave the squishy one to its fate."

"Can I take a picture of it?" I ask, checking tomatoes off my list.

My mom looks at me like I'm nuts. "Whatever for?"

"I'm going to put *everything* in my project — pictures of rotten tomatoes, stacks of potatoes, and Jasmine riding on the shopping cart!"

I take a disposable camera from my sack and snap a close-up of the disgusting tomato. Then Jasmine jumps on the back of the cart and I take a picture of her waving and holding a stinky onion to her nose.

"Get some lettuce," Mom says.

I grab a round green thing that looks like a giant, leafy softball.

"That's cabbage!" Mom tells me. "Lettuce looks similar, but it's not as heavy. Cabbage on sandwiches is pretty awful."

"My bad!" I tell her as I make the switch.

Jasmine and I then pick out blueberries, raspberries, and blackberries in little plastic cartons. We place them carefully in the cart.

"I think we better wait on the berries, Sassy," my mother says.

"How come?"

"Berries go bad really quickly."

"But I'm going to make the food ahead of time," I protest.

"Okay, but don't say I didn't warn you."

When we get to the strawberries, I tell Jasmine, "I'm making little mice out of strawberries! If you close your eyes, can you imagine a little mousy nose on the pointed front of one of these?"

Jasmine tries. "Not really. I have to see you do it. What are you going to use for a tail?"

"Red string licorice!" I tell her with glee.

"Ooh, yummy."

"You should spend the night at my house on Friday. We can make the little strawberry mice."

"Ooh, yeah! Can I, Mrs. Sanford? I can help Sassy do lots of stuff to get ready."

"Sure. I'll call your mom this afternoon."

Jasmine and I hook pinkies and wink.

We add kiwi and grapes and peaches to our shopping cart. I take a picture of Jasmine sneaking a taste of a grape, and she takes a picture of me sticking a banana in my ear.

Mom shakes her head and tries to pretend she doesn't know us.

We get walnuts and granola and almonds from the health food aisle. We find chocolate chips and chocolate topping and licorice from the not-so-healthy part of the store. We also find ice cream and yogurt and several kinds of pudding. And cheese. Lots of cheese.

"Which package of chunk cheese should I get, Mom?" I ask her.

"Which one gives you more cheese per ounce for the price?" she answers.

"I don't know. I'd need math for that!" I complain.

"Well, start figuring," she says.

I look at the prices carefully. I do some calculating in my head. Finally, I pick the big package of chunk cheese. The package is decorated in plain black and white. Boring but cheaper.

"Good job, Sassy!" Mom says, nodding her head in approval. "This one is the best buy!"

"Don't tell Mr. Olsen I did that," I tell Jasmine. "He'd never believe it!"

"You got it. I hate it when teachers are right," she says. We continue down the aisles.

"Ooh! Look!" I cry out. I stop at a display of ice cube trays and cookie cutters in all kinds of different shapes. Triangles and animals and even worms. Exactly what I need!

"Get the one that looks like a snake!" Jasmine suggests eagerly. "And the dragon one!"

I grab several more. A bear. A star. A kangaroo. A palm tree. Awesome.

Our cart is filling up fast.

"You've got mostly dessert foods," Mom observes. "What about the main meal part of your feast?"

"I almost forgot!" I go back to my list, which has lots of ingredients checked off in purple marker. We take the cart to the lunch meat section.

"Chicken!" I say, reading from the list.

"Check," Jasmine says as she grabs a package of sliced chicken.

"Turkey."

"Check, but what's the difference?"

"I think it tastes better," I tell her.

"Okay. Check."

"Ham."

"Check."

"Roast beef?"

"Check."

"No, get that brand instead," Mom says. "I have a coupon for it."

"Okay. What about bologna?" Jasmine asks.

"Oh, yes! To make bologna bowls!" I tell her. "Get three packages!"

"You've got *me* making those things at my house!" Jasmine tells me.

"And aren't you glad I did?"

Mom has a coupon for bologna. She finds a clipping for several other items in our cart.

We also get jam and jelly and food coloring. Bread and milk and several kinds of juice. Popsicle sticks and paper plates and napkins. Our cart is getting heavy.

I take a picture of the stuffed cart. Mom's face looks serious as we get to the checkout. She pulls out her coupons and hands them to the checkout lady.

I give the lady our reusable bags.

As the woman slides each item across the scanner, Jasmine and I check out the rack of candy and bubble gum right next to us.

"Mom, can I —"

"Not a chance," she says before I can finish.

Jasmine and I look at each other knowingly. We know when to push a mom and when to shut up. So we don't say anything else about candy.

When the total amount is tallied, Mom sighs and slides her credit card through the machine. "Oo-wee! I sure hope this party is worth it," she says.

"I *promise*, Mom. I'm going to do it all myself. Well, Jasmine is going to help me, but we're going to make you proud. Nothing will go wrong. Promise. Promise. Promise."

I snap a picture of Mom as she rubs her forehead. That's a sure sign that she is worried.

We roll our heavy cart out to the car.

CHAPTER TEN

Cooking in a Thunderstorm

When I get home from school on Monday, even though it is raining outside, I'm in a terrific mood. Lillian can come to the party! I place her RSVP on our refrigerator door with a pink, shiny butterfly magnet that I found in my sack.

"Mom! Can I start making stuff for the party?" I ask.

"Have you done your homework?" Mom always asks that question.

"This *is* my homework!" I tell her.

"Which recipe are you going to make first?" she asks me.

"The frozen stuff," I tell her. "It can stay in the freezer all week."

"Tell me what you're going to do," she says.

"I call this one Sassy's Red Frozen Sparkle Sickles," I tell her. "I have decided to give every recipe a name. I'm going to give the kids a menu when they get here. Just like in a real restaurant."

"Do you need my help?" Mom asks.

"I don't think so," I reply.

"I'll just sit here at the table and read the newspaper, okay? You go right ahead." Mom opens the newspaper and acts like she is ignoring me. But I know she is watching.

I get my recipe list from my Sassy Sack and get out each ingredient. Pineapple juice and fruit punch from the refrigerator. Applesauce and crushed pineapple from the cupboard. Sugar.

"I really like these cool-shaped ice cube trays we got," I say as I remove their plastic coverings. "Should I use the blue bowl?" I ask Mom. I also find her measuring cup.

"The red one is bigger," she comments without looking up.

I pull the red one from the cupboard, and just as I'm ready to open the bottle of pincapple juice, Mom says, "Wash your hands, Sassy. And be sure to shake the juice before you pour it."

I sorta want her to leave me alone, but I'm kinda glad she's sitting there. I wash my hands, shake the juice, and open the bottle.

I measure out one cup of the pineapple juice. I pour it

carefully into the bowl. Not one drop spills. Then I measure one cup of the fruit punch and add that to it. It looks delicious.

"What do I do with the leftover fruit punch?" I ask Mom as I replace the top.

Sabin barges into the room. "I'll drink it, Sassy!" he says loudly. He reaches for the fruit punch.

"No, Sabin!" I cry out. I snatch the bottle from him. "I might need more. Drink some soda instead. But not the one in the green bottle. That's for my party."

Sabin makes a face, but he grabs something else to drink. Then he puts a spoon into the freshly opened jar of apple-sauce. "Yummy!" he declares.

"Sabin, quit!" I tell him. "I need that for my recipe! Mom, make him stop messing with my stuff!"

Mom looks up from her paper. "Give your sister a break, Sabin," she says. "If you let her finish making everything, I'm sure she'll let you sample the finished products."

"Okay. Okay." Sabin opens a package of cookies. "Are you using these, too?"

"No. Help yourself."

He takes about five of them, then saunters out of the kitchen.

I glance out the kitchen window. It's really dark out, even though it's still early afternoon. I hear thunder rumbling in the distance. But that's far away, and I'm here in Mom's kitchen, and I'm rocking!

I take a deep breath. "Where was I?" I say out loud. I add the applesauce and crushed pineapple to the mixture in the bowl, and about a quarter cup of sugar.

I stir and stir and stir. I taste a little with my finger. Heavenly! And it really does look sparkly. Just perfect for me!

I rinse the funny-shaped ice trays. Very carefully, I pour the red sparkle mixture into containers shaped like stars and animals.

I pull my camera from my Sassy Sack. I take a picture of the shimmery red stuff in the trays. I can't wait to eat a Sparkle Sickle!

Then I open the freezer.

"Mom!" I tell her. "There's no room in here!"

"Move some stuff around, Sassy. Take that roast out — I'll make it for dinner tomorrow. Then arrange everything else so you have a free shelf."

It's cold in the freezer. Really cold. By the time I finish, my fingers are almost numb. But I carefully place my molds and close the door. One recipe down. A million more to go.

Being a famous chef is hard work!

"Can I make my pie next?" I ask Mom. "It goes in the freezer also. This one is called Sassy's Orange Supreme Frozen Pie."

"Go for it," Mom says. She is working on a crossword puzzle.

This time I get out a graham cracker crust. It is already made and stuck to a pie pan. "Cool!" I say.

Then I laugh to myself because the next thing I take out of the freezer is the Cool Whip.

Next I get out a can of mandarin orange slices and a couple of containers of orange yogurt.

I rinse a bowl, and this time I pour in the yogurt and the topping and stir it up. The color is a pale orange, and it tastes soft and light and creamy.

"Don't forget to drain the juice from your oranges," Mom warns me. "You need the sieve."

"I know, I know," I tell her. But I really had forgotten. I would have had a soupy, sloppy mess in the bowl.

I drain the juice into a little bowl full of holes, called a sieve. I think *sieve* is a funny word. It sure is a funny-looking bowl. I toss the oranges into the mixture. I stir for a couple of minutes, then pour it into the pie crust.

"Easy breezy!" I say out loud.

I snap another photo. This one looks like an orange cloud.

I cover the pie with aluminum foil. One more recipe in the freezer. I'm doing great!

More thunder rumbles. It's getting closer. I see flashes of lightning.

"Okay, Sassy," Mom says. "Wash your utensils now and let me make dinner. You've done a great job."

"I told you I could do this, Mom," I tell her proudly.

"So far, so good," she says.

I hardly ever volunteer to wash the dishes, but I carefully rinse my bowl and spoons and clear away all my trash.

The rain is coming down really hard outside.

Sadora rushes into the kitchen, her hair dripping and her clothes soaked. Daddy is right behind her.

"What a mess!" she cries out. "I got drenched just running from the car!"

"You ought to see your hair," I tell her.

She runs to the hall mirror. "Eek! What if somebody sees me like this?"

Mom and Daddy look at each other and roll their eyes.

Sadora rushes upstairs to fix her hair.

I help Mom set the table. It's getting darker and darker outside.

Thunder booms and lightning flashes.

"It looks like nighttime," I say to Mom.

Sabin is in the family room, playing a video game. I can

hear Sadora's blow dryer upstairs. Mom pops a casserole into the microwave. Daddy dries his face and hair with a towel, then clicks on his favorite news show.

That's when another huge flash of lightning brightens the dark sky outside. Suddenly, the whole house goes dark.

The microwave stops. The blow dryer goes silent. The newsman on TV halts in midsentence. Sabin's game stops beeping.

Everything has lost power.

CHAPTER ELEVEN

What Should I Wear to My Party?

"What happened?" Sadora cries as she runs down the steps in her bare feet.

"It seems the electrical storm has knocked out a power line," Daddy says.

"But what about my hair? I didn't get to finish drying and styling it!"

"It's dark. Nobody can see you," Mom says, chuckling.

It's not completely dark, but it's really gloomy and scary. Especially with all the thunder and lightning.

Sabin's dog, Zero, whimpers every time it thunders.

I find my sack and pull out three small flashlights. I click on one and I give the other two to Sadora and Sabin. He shines his light on Zero, then sits on the floor with him.

"This reminds me of the time we were in the hurricane at Grammy's house," I whisper into the dim light.

"Yes, but this is no hurricane, Sassy," Mom says. Her voice makes me feel better.

Mom digs through the kitchen drawers and finds a couple of large flashlights. She also pulls out some candles. She sets them on the table and lights them. The glow looks special and makes me feel safe.

"Sit down, kids," Daddy says. "We can still have a good dinner. Plus, thanks to Sassy, my boom box works, and we can have music as well as candlelight for our dinner."

"Daddy's music is like listening to the greatest hits of three centuries ago," Sadora teases.

"What are we gonna eat, Mom?" Sabin asks.

"I guess we'll just have sandwiches." Mom turns to me. "Sassy, we're going to need some of the lunch meat we bought for your party. We'll get some more before Saturday. Don't worry."

There is nothing I can do, so Mom makes sandwiches from my turkey and cheese. At least she doesn't use my cool cookie cutters. Our meal is just ordinary. Except it's in the dark. And it's using my special food. And Daddy's old-fashioned, battery-operated boom box is playing softly in the background.

At least my pie and my Sparkle Sickles are safe. But then I think: *The refrigerator is off! My recipes are going to melt!*

What a disaster!

"Mom!" I screech. "What about my creations in the freezer?"

"For your party? What did you make?" Sadora asks.

"Sassy's Red Frozen Sparkle Sickles and Sassy's Orange Supreme Frozen Pie!" I tell her.

"You named them?" She shakes her head in wonder.

"Well, yeah! I created a name for every single one of my recipes. And those two are melting!"

"Calm down, Sassy," Daddy says. "The refrigerator will stay cold for several hours. Your special desserts won't melt for awhile."

"But what if the lights don't come back on soon? At Grammy's house it took a couple of days!"

"This is just a thunderstorm," Mom says in a soothing voice. "The power will be restored by morning. Trust me."

She was right.

The next morning the lights are blazing and I hear the sound of the blow dryer in the bathroom.

I get up and start to get dressed for school. Boring blue-and-white uniform once more.

But then I stop and think. *What should I wear for my dazzling dinner party? Something dazzling, of course!*

I check my closet. Let's see. The first thing I find is a pink sun visor that Grammy sent me a couple of months ago. It is decorated with silver sparkles. I love it! It's just so very Sassy! Grammy knows what I like. But I decide not to wear it for the party. I think it will be better for a picnic.

Hmm. I see a blue-striped shirt I haven't worn in a long time. I try it on. Perfect! And it's got silver sparkles all over the front. Even better. I pull a silver belt from my Sassy Sack. It adds just the right touch.

Hot-pink capri pants. Blue socks. White tennis shoes. I set my outfit aside and place it carefully in my top drawer. Zero has a reputation for gobbling socks. I have to be careful.

Then I hurry to get on my un-sparkly uniform and get downstairs for breakfast.

"Are my desserts okay?" I ask Mom before I even say good morning.

"Yes, Sassy. They are fine. The power came back on around midnight. But I think you forgot something."

"What?" I ask.

"Aren't your Sparkle Sickles supposed to be something like Popsicles?"

"Yes."

"I think you forgot to add the Popsicle sticks!" she says.

"Oh, no!" I put my hand to my mouth. "What should I do, Mom?"

"It's not the end of the world, Sassy," Mom says calmly.

"When you get home from school, take them out for an hour or so. When they start to melt a little, insert your sticks and then pop them back in the freezer."

"Are you sure that will work?" I ask.

"Great chefs always have secrets," she tells me with a wink.

I feel better. A little. There is so much to remember. And the time for the party is getting closer.

It's hard to sit through school because I'm so excited. I keep checking my list and thinking about recipes, not our social studies chapter on Peru.

Just before the bell rings to go home, Lillian asks me softly, "How many people are coming to the party, Sassy?"

"Fifteen, including you," I tell her. "I'm so glad you're coming."

She smiles brightly. It is not her usual sad smile. "I hope to have a surprise for everybody on Saturday," she tells me.

"Awesome! What is it?"

"It's a secret. I think it's pretty cool. That's all I can say right now."

We head out the door together. Lillian walks to her limo. I climb onto my school bus. We wave good-bye.

Mom takes me to school each morning, but I take the bus home. Jasmine and I always sit together.

"I wonder what Lillian's surprise is," I ask Jasmine as I sit down next to her.

"If you knew, it wouldn't be a surprise, right?" Jasmine says.

"I suppose."

"Do you have any gum?" Jasmine asks.

"Do you even have to ask?" I reply. "What flavor?"

"Tutti-frutti!" she says.

I dig down into my sack and pull out a pack of fruit gum and a pack of double-bubble berry gum as well. Jasmine takes a piece of each and stuffs both in her mouth.

But the gum just makes me think about my berry recipes and the purple milk shakes I'm planning. My head is stuffed with food!

CHAPTER TWELVE
The Party Is Tomorrow!

I can't believe the party is tomorrow! I have worked every night this week, making dishes and making plans.

Tuesday after school I practiced making strawberry mice. Mom was right. Strawberries get icky and squishy very fast. And the red raspberries I bought turned black! With white mold growing all over them. I had to throw them away. I hate that.

Wednesday I worked a little on my menus. I will hand them out to people when they get here.

Thursday I helped Mom clean up. I hid Sabin's shoes, which are always in the middle of the floor. I ran the vacuum. I dusted the furniture. I don't think fourth-grade kids care if the coffee table is dusty. But Mom cares, so I do my very best.

Jasmine is sleeping over tonight. We have lots to do.

"What's first?" Jasmine says with excitement. We are

both wearing jeans and old T-shirts. It always feels good to take off that uniform.

"Let's see," I reply. "When kids get here, we will give them recipes to prepare."

"That's going to be fun," Jasmine says.

"And messy!" I laugh as I pull my list from my sack. "Okay. Tandy, Iris, and Basima will make Sassy's Dazzling Banana Chocolate Sprinkle Delight."

"How about on this side of the kitchen counter?" Jasmine suggests.

"Great idea. Over there we will put the bananas, the chocolate topping, and the sprinkles and stuff."

"Ooey, gooey!" Jasmine says, and gets the ingredients and places them in that corner.

"Then Carmelita, Misty, Holly, and Josephina can make Sassy's Technicolor Fruit on a Stick on the other end of the counter."

"I think it's so cool that you have named everything, Sassy," Jasmine says. "What will the boys make?"

"I think I want them to make the milk shakes," I tell her. "What can go wrong?"

"Don't ask!"

"No disasters allowed!" We both laugh. Then I ask her, "Do you think you and Lillian can make the strawberry mice? I don't want them to get messed up."

"Oh, yes! That will be super!" Jasmine exclaims.

"I want her to have a good time. I don't think she gets to go to many parties," I say.

"You are probably right." Then Jasmine asks, "Who will make the sandwiches?"

"The bread and lunch meat and cheese will be on the kitchen table. With the cool cookie cutters. And ketchup and mustard and other fixings. Each person makes his or her own."

"So what do we do now?" Jasmine asks.

I take a deep breath. "The most elegant and special item on the menu," I reply with excitement. "Sassy's Amazing Kaleidoscope No-Bake Fruit Pizza."

"What's a kaleidoscope?" Jasmine asks.

"It's still one of my favorite toys from when I was little," I explain. "It's a long tube. When you look through it, you can see stones and sparkles. Every time you move the dial, you get another beautiful design."

"Sounds like a real Sassy toy," she says.

"You want to see it?" I ask her.

"Yeah!"

I reach for my sack and push my hand down to the very bottom. I feel it with my fingers. I pull it out. "My kaleidoscope," I say simply.

Jasmine takes it and holds it up to the light. "Wow!"

"Turn the dial."

"Even better. Awesome! It's like diamonds and jewels and magic!"

"It's always a different design. It's never the same and I never get tired of looking at it."

"I can see why," she says as she hands it back to me.

"That's why I named this pizza after my kaleidoscope. It's going to be amazing."

"Well, let's get started," Jasmine says. Her eyes are glowing. She knows what a big deal this one is.

I get out the pizza pan, the cream cheese, and all the fruit. Mom bought more fruit. She didn't even say, "I told you so."

"Start slicing the fruit," I tell Jasmine. "You don't need a sharp knife."

"Into chunks?" Jasmine asks.

"Try thin slices. Think of it as fruit pepperoni."

"Gotcha!"

I mix a little apricot jam with water. "This will stop the fruit from turning brown," I tell Jasmine.

"How do you know all this stuff?" she asks.

"Mom told me about how to save the fruit. But I invented the recipe myself. After doing lots of research on the Internet."

"I guess that's what Miss Armstrong wanted us to do," she says.

She slices the strawberries and combines them with the blueberries and raspberries and blackberries. Her fingers are covered with berry slime.

I help her as I slice the bananas and kiwi and peaches, and open the can of pineapple chunks. Then I cover the fruit with the jam-and-water mixture.

"What's next?" she asks.

I wash my hands at the kitchen sink. "We mix the graham cracker crumbs with the cream cheese and butter. With our hands!"

"Let's do it!"

We mix the stuff together. The cream cheese gets under my fingernails. We spread it on the pan.

"It looks like a real pizza crust!" Jasmine says with surprise. "What is the next layer?"

"Apple jelly!"

"Sweet!"

We spread the jelly over the whole thing, then add a layer of Cool Whip. Mom comes into the kitchen.

"How's it going, girls?"

"We're on it, Mom!"

"Let me have your camera, Sassy," she says. "You really need a picture of this!"

"It's in my sack. On the right-hand side, in the outside

pocket," I tell her. My hands are still covered with sweet stuff.

Mom finds the camera and snaps several photos. In one picture Jasmine and I have both our hands covered with Cool Whip. Then Mom takes a snapshot of the mountain of fruit we have sliced.

"You two are doing a great job," Mom says. She leaves us in the kitchen.

"Okay, time to place the fruit," I tell Jasmine. Very carefully, we make a circle of berries and bananas and kiwi and peaches and canned pineapple chunks. Each fruit gets its own circle.

When we finish, it really does look a little like a kaleidoscope. I feel very proud. We snap several photos.

"What do with we do with all this leftover fruit and ingredients?" Jasmine asks.

"You know what? I think we should make another one!"

"You're right, so that each person gets a taste."

So we take all the leftovers and do it again. The second fruit pizza is a little lopsided. And not quite as pretty as the first one. But at least we will have enough for everyone.

I take one more picture. We place both of the fruit pizzas in the refrigerator.

We clear the table, wipe it off, and wash the dishes.

"This is really hard work!" Jasmine says as she mops her forehead.

"I never thought about how hard it is to be a mom," I tell her. "She has to do stuff like this every day."

"Yep. I'm glad I'm a kid."

We stop and sip from a couple of juice boxes.

"Let's print out these menus and get to bed," I suggest.

"I'm with you!" Jasmine agrees.

We head to the family room. Mom is reading a book. Daddy is asleep in his big chair. Sabin is outside shooting hoops by the garage door. Sadora is at school. I think she has play practice.

"Can we use more of that purple paper?" I ask Mom. "I just need to print out my menus."

"Sure," Mom says. She loads the machine with the lavender paper. I find my menu and click on it. Then I hit PRINT.

The first one rolls from the machine. At the top it reads, *Sassy's Dazzling Dinner Party.* Everything I am serving is listed neatly. It's like a menu in a restaurant.

Jasmine looks at it. "This looks great, Sassy. But if you are going to ask kids to make some of the food, you need to tell them what to do."

"You're right!" I tell her. "I need to print out my recipes, too! I'm so glad you're here, Jasmine."

"Be sure to write down the names of each kid next to the meal he or she will prepare," she reminds me.

"Another great idea!"

I print out fifteen menus. Then I print out fifteen copies of the recipes. I include the names of kids. That one takes two pages. At the top, the words say, *Sassy's Delicious and Delightful Recipes*.

"We're using up all your mom's purple ink," Jasmine notices.

"Print what you need to, girls," Mom says. "But don't overdo it."

"Okay, Mom," I tell her.

We place the recipes and menus neatly on the family room table.

"Should we decorate them?" Jasmine asks.

"Glitter ink!" I reply with glee. "And stickers!" I reach down into my Sassy Sack and pull out a handful of glitter pens and a small booklet of shiny stickers. I give the pink and silver pens to Jasmine. I keep the purple and gold ones. We share the sticker book.

We add glossy flowers and fruit and star stickers to each menu, then color around each one with the glitter pens. Then we decorate each copy of the recipes with more metallic stickers and glittery decorations. The result is glorious!

I check the kitchen once more before we go to bed. The purple paper plates and pink napkins are stacked neatly in one corner. Two huge rolls of paper towels wait to clean up any messes. Ingredients and bowls wait to be used.

The kids will start arriving at three o'clock tomorrow. Everything should be over by six.

We are ready.

CHAPTER THIRTEEN
Almost Disaster

I wake up Saturday morning feeling giddy and happy. I see sunshine outside my window. No rain today. Good.

Jasmine, waking up in the other twin bed, looks at me and grins. "Today is the day!" she says. She sits up. Her hair is a mess.

"Let's get dressed!" I suggest. I am shivering with excitement.

My hair is a bigger mess that Jasmine's. While she is in the bathroom, I try my best to tame my tangles. I use a brush and a comb and lots of hair gel. It's still pretty wild.

I slip on my blue-striped sparkly shirt and pink capris. The silver belt is perfect. It highlights my shirt and I like the way I look in the mirror. I sling my purple sparkly sack over my shoulder. Perfect!

Jasmine is wearing mostly lavender today. She has purple

plaid shorts and a pale pink T-shirt. She looks great, except she's barefoot.

"I can't find my socks!" she says. "I have brand-new purple socks. My mom bought them the other day."

We look under the bed and in the closet. The socks are gone.

I have a terrible thought. I open my bedroom door and yell into the hall, "Sabin! Where is your dog?"

Sabin doesn't answer, but Zero trots into my room. His tongue is purple. In his mouth are shreds of a purple sock.

"Your dog ate my socks?" Jasmine asks, amazed. "I don't believe it!"

"He's Sabin's dog. But I should have warned you about the socks. That dog is nutso!"

I chase Zero out of my room. He wags his tail as if nothing bad has happened. I am trying not to get upset. There is too much to do today.

I give Jasmine a pair of my own socks. They are white with little purple decorations on the top.

"I guess I better put them on quickly," she says. "I've never seen a dog that eats clothes!"

We head downstairs for breakfast. Sabin is sitting at the kitchen table, eating a banana dipped in chocolate. He has dripped chocolate on the floor.

"Sabin! What are you doing?" I cry out.

"Testing your recipe!" he says. "This chocolate and banana stuff is dynamite."

"You're not supposed to eat my special food ahead of time!" I wail. "It's for my guests!"

"Relax, Sassy," he says. "You've got plenty left." He points to a huge pile of bananas on the counter. "Mom and I went to the store early this morning to get more stuff for your party."

"You did?"

"Yep!"

"You got up early on a Saturday?"

"Yep." He finishes his banana.

I decide not to yell at him about Zero eating Jasmine's socks.

We eat a quick breakfast of cold cereal and hot chocolate, then go outside to snap pictures of each other in our cute outfits.

When we come back in, Jasmine and I go into the family room. Every single one of my recipe sheets and menus are on the floor. They are ripped and chewed. They are torn. Muddy paw prints cover most of them.

"Sabin!" I scream once more. "Look what your dog has done!"

"Oh, snap. My bad." Sabin rushes in to pick up the tattered purple papers.

"They're ruined!" I am trying not to cry.

"Let's print some more, Sassy," Jasmine says gently. "Look, the purple paper is still loaded in the machine."

"But what about all our extra decorations with the stickers and glitter pens?" I wail as we toss most of the menus in the trash.

"If I know you, Sassy, you have plenty more glitter pens and shiny stickers hiding in that super sack of yours. Right?"

I frown, but she's right. I've got plenty of that stuff hidden down in my Sassy Sack.

While Jasmine and Sabin pick up the rest of the messed-up menus, I reprint everything.

Then Jasmine and I add stickers and purple and pink glitter ink around each one. It takes a long time. I think the first time we did it, everything looked better. But we finish them all. This time I place the stack on the highest shelf I can reach in the family room.

"Please," I beg Sabin. "Don't let Zero ruin my party. Can you keep him tied up when the kids get here?"

He puts his arm around me. "Okay. I promise." He whistles for the dog. "Come on, Zero. We have to make you disappear." They both head upstairs to Sabin's room.

In the kitchen, I find that Mom has bought more fresh

strawberries and bananas and raspberries, plus plastic forks and spoons. I had totally forgotten about those.

"After everybody makes their recipes, where do we eat?" Jasmine asks.

"In the family room and the dining room," I tell her. "Daddy is setting up folding chairs, plus kids can sit on the floor."

When Sadora comes downstairs, she smiles at me and Jasmine. "You two look cute!"

"Thanks," we say at the same time.

"Ooh! I've got something for you!" She runs back upstairs. Jasmine and I look at each other.

Sadora returns, carrying a purple visor in her hand. "Here, Jasmine," she says. "Try this on and see what you think."

"Wow! Thanks, Sadora!" Jasmine slips the visor over her hair. Even though I'd thought my pink visor wouldn't be right for a dinner party, Sadora's purple visor looks great on Jasmine and fits perfectly. That's when I see that a visor can work for all kinds of special events, even this one.

"You can have it," Sadora says with a smile. "It looks great with your outfit."

"Thanks so much!" Jasmine says. She runs to the mirror to check it out.

"I heard what Zero did to your socks." Sadora chuckles.

I give Sadora a big hug. "You're the best!" I whisper.

"I've got play practice this morning, but I'll be back in time for your party. Break a leg!"

"Huh?"

"When you're in a play, that's what people say to wish you good luck," she explains.

"Oh! Okay. I'm nervous enough without worrying about broken bones!"

Daddy takes her to play practice, and we are left in the kitchen alone.

I check my goodies in the freezer. They look perfect.

I check my fruit pizzas. One is still lumpy, but they are ready.

"I guess there's nothing left to do but wait," I tell Jasmine.

"I have an idea," Jasmine suggests. "We have extra time. We have extra bananas. So let's make Jasmine's Famous Creamy Banana Pudding!"

"Now you're naming *your* recipes!"

"If you can do it, so can I," she answers. "Actually, it's my mom's recipe, but we make it together all the time."

"What ingredients do we need?" I ask her.

"Do you have vanilla wafers and banana pudding?"

I check Mom's cupboard. "Yes and yes. What do we do first?"

"Ask your mom."

"Smart cookie!" I tell her. "Mom!" I call upstairs. "Can me and Jasmine make some banana pudding for the party?"

"Do you need the stove?" she calls back.

"Nope!"

"Okay. Go ahead. Be careful," she answers. Moms always add that *be careful* line.

"What do we do now?" I ask Jasmine.

"You slice the bananas and I'll make the pudding. We need milk."

I get a gallon of milk from the refrigerator. The shelves are a little high for me because I'm so short, but I manage to get it out without spilling.

I carefully peel and slice the bananas and lay them like little soldiers around the inside of Mom's red bowl.

"Oops! You have to line the bowl with the cookies first," Jasmine tells me.

"You didn't tell me." I take out the bananas. They feel squishy in my hand. Then I line the bowl with the vanilla wafers. Of course I eat quite a few while I'm doing it. Then I place several banana slices on top of each cookie. One at a time.

Then another layer of cookies. And another layer of banana slices.

Jasmine makes the pudding by adding milk to the powder and stirring really fast.

"Whew!" she says.

She then pours the sweet, slightly lumpy banana pudding over the cookies and bananas. We top it off with more cookies. We gobble a few as we finish.

"You got room in the refrigerator for one more bowl?" she asks.

"Just barely."

We cover the bowl with plastic wrap and place it in the fridge.

We set out all the ingredients on the table and the counters.

It's almost time.

We play Scrabble in the family room while we check our watches. Jasmine wins one game and I win one. The phone rings.

I pick it up to answer. "Oh, hi, Carmelita. Yes, we are still starting at three. You're wearing your new dress? Awesome! I can't wait to see it."

Carmelita asks another question.

"Sure, you can bring a treat! Peanut butter balls! Perfect! Tell your mom I said thanks."

I hang up the phone. "Carmelita's bringing more goodies!" I tell Jasmine. "We are going to have *so* much food!"

"Sounds good to me," Jasmine says.

Sadora comes home from play practice. "I'm going upstairs to get my camera, Sassy," she tells me. "I'll snap photos of everything!"

"Thanks, Sadora," I whisper. "And tell Sabin to keep Zero upstairs, okay?"

"Gotcha!"

CHAPTER FOURTEEN
The Kitchen Is Purple!

At exactly three o'clock, my doorbell rings. Jasmine and I slap palms and run to open the door. Travis stands there with his mom. He looks a little nervous. He is wearing a white shirt and a red tie.

My mother comes downstairs and greets them. "Thanks so much for coming!" Mom says.

"Travis and I made his favorite pudding to share with the kids," his mom tells my mom. "I hope you don't mind."

"Oh, not at all," my mother says. "I'm sure these kids will eat everything that's not tied down!"

Travis's mom promises to pick him up at six. He looks glad when she leaves. He takes his tie off as soon as her car is out of the driveway.

He comes into the kitchen carrying a large plastic bag.

"I brought dirt pudding," he says.

"Awesome!" Jasmine says. "I love dirt pudding!"

"Me, too," I tell him. "Chocolate cookies crunched into chocolate pudding! Yummy!"

"Don't forget the worms!" he reminds us. "It's stuffed with gummy worms." He removes a large bowl from the bag. He sets it on the table.

Sadora, true to her word, snaps a photo of the brown, gooey pudding. I think she gets a close-up of a worm sticking out.

"You're the first one here," I tell him.

"Not for long!" Jasmine says. She is looking out my front window. "I see Carmelita and Josephina! And right behind them are Holly and Misty."

The four girls come in noisily. All four are wearing dresses.

"You didn't get dressed up," Misty says to me. "You said it was an *elegant* party!"

"You look charming!" Sadora says. They seem to like a compliment from a real teenager. She takes a picture of the four of them.

"As long as I can wear sparkles and not a uniform, I feel elegant," I tell Misty.

"You're right. I love getting dressed up, and we never really have a chance during the week."

Carmelita places her peanut butter balls on the kitchen table. It is quickly getting crowded.

Travis glances out the window. "All right!" he says. "I see the rest of the guys! I was afraid I was going to have to talk about sparkles and dresses all afternoon!"

Rusty, Ricky, Charles, and Abdul have come in Rusty's parents' car.

The house is getting crowded, too.

Jasmine gives each person a menu and a recipe sheet.

"Nice decorations," Carmelita says. She touches the shiny stickers and gives me a nod.

"Thanks," I tell her. "Jasmine and I worked really hard on the decorations. Twice!"

Jasmine adds, "Sassy's brother has a dog with purple decorations stuck in his teeth!" Everybody laughs.

Just as I start to explain what to do, Tandy, Iris, Princess, and Basima arrive one after the other. Kids are in the kitchen. Kids are in the family room.

Princess has to go to the bathroom. Sadora takes pictures of everything.

My mom stands on the bottom step keeping her eye on things. But she does not interfere.

The only person who is not here is Lillian. I am a little worried. But I decide to get started anyway.

I stand up on a kitchen chair. "Welcome to my dazzling dinner party," I tell them all. I hold my arms up high. Sadora snaps a photo.

"This is the first party I've been to that's not for a birthday," Misty says. "No presents."

"Nope, it's not my birthday," I tell them. "This started out as a project for Miss Armstrong. But it ended being just plain fun."

"So when do we eat?" Rusty asks.

Everybody laughs.

"You eat when you finish preparing your meal!" I explain.

"What?"

"You're really gonna make us cook?"

"I've never been to a party where I have to cook my own food!"

"I like the idea!" Princess says. "We all have something to do and we all get to eat everybody's creations."

I smile to thank her.

I hold my hand up so everybody will listen. "I already made a bunch of stuff. But check the purple menu sheet. Your name is written next to your recipe. Tandy, Iris, and Basima, you get to make Sassy's Dazzling Banana Chocolate Sprinkle Delight. All the stuff you need is right over there."

"Cool!" they say.

"Carmelita, Misty, Holly, and Josephina. You get to make Sassy's Technicolor Fruit on a Stick at the other end of the counter."

"Sounds easy enough," Misty says.

"Yep. Basically you're just sticking fruit onto a stick. I've already cut it up for you."

Those four girls move toward the fruit.

"Princess, can you make the soda? We have bubble-gum pink and bubble-gum blue. It's just clear juice and food coloring and sherbet!"

"Sure, Sassy!"

"The cups are over there," I say, pointing.

"What about us?" a couple of the boys ask.

"You get to make Sassy's Purple Passion Milk Shake. You get to use the blender. But my mom will have a horse if you make a mess," I warn them.

"We got this!" Travis and Rusty say.

"And Sassy's Glamorous Green Shake-a-Pudding. Add the green stuff, shake, and pour."

"I can do that!" Abdul yells.

"Okay! As soon as we get this done, we make our sandwiches. Then we feast!"

For a minute, everything works perfectly. Almost.

Jasmine starts to make a strawberry mouse. She adds the

almond chips for its ears and the chocolate chips for its eyes and nose. She sticks the licorice into its back for the tail. Almost like magic, a mouse appears.

Rusty and Ricky are pretending to be pirates. They are using the fruit skewers for swords.

Tandy drops the bottle of chocolate sauce. A huge brown glob lands on the floor. I rush over with paper towels.

Charles and Abdul squirt each other with cans of whipped cream.

Misty bumps Basima's arm. Crunchy sprinkles from the bowl Basima is holding flutter to the floor. On top of the chocolate. More paper towels.

Travis shakes up the bottle of 7-Up as he hands it to Princess.

I try to warn her, but she opens it too quickly. She is standing right next to Charles. He looks really surprised when cold soda sprays him in the face. More paper towels.

But everybody is laughing and having fun. Sadora takes snapshots of it all.

The bubble-gum soda looks awesome. Princess must have put a whole bunch of food coloring in the juice. With the strawberry sherbet floating on top, it looks like a weird pink ocean.

"You got strawberries and soda hidden down in that sack of yours?" Carmelita asks as she gobbles a banana.

"No, but almost everything else," I tell her as I pull a package of candy sprinkles and a box of marbles from my sack.

"I understand the sprinkles, but what's with the marbles?" she asks.

"I want you to put them in those drinking glasses," I explain.

"You want us to drink marbles?"

"Of course not, silly. That's where you and Misty and Holly and Josephina will place the fruit on skewers. The marbles will keep the fruit sticks in place."

Carmelita nods with understanding. "You've got it together, Sassy! The fruit sticks will look like flower bouquets when we're done. Awesome!" She hurries over to the girls with the marbles.

Jasmine and I get out the lunch meat and bread and fixings. We line up the cookie cutters so kids can cut their food into shapes. I place the meat in a fancy circle on a large tray. A slice of turkey. A slice of ham. Then chicken. Then beef. In between each I place a slice of cheese. It looks pretty when I finish. I set the tray near the edge of the kitchen table. There is no other room.

I make a couple of sample sandwiches. I use the dragon-shaped cutter and end up with a dragon sandwich!

"Cool!" I say.

Lillian still has not arrived.

Travis and Rusty start to make the purple milk shake. They pour everything into the blender. Travis puts the top on the blender. Rusty is ready to push the button to start it.

I check the window. Finally, I see a limo pulling up to our house. It seems bigger than usual. But maybe that's because we have never had a limo in our driveway!

Lillian is finally here!

I rush to the door to greet her.

At the same time, Zero rushes down the steps.

He seems excited to see so many kids in the house. He runs into the kitchen and greets each kid.

Zero loves to eat. Socks. And food. So he sniffs and sniffs as he lets the kids pet him.

"Where is Sabin?" I ask Sadora.

"I don't know." She laughs as she takes a million pictures of the dog in the kitchen.

"Get Zero out of here!" I hiss.

Mom calls out from the family room, "Come here, Zero!"

But Zero is too excited to listen. He sniffs the kitchen table. He puts one paw on the edge of my lovely meat tray. All the meat topples to the floor and Zero gobbles it as fast as he can.

"Oh, no!" I cry out.

The doorbell rings.

I open it and see Lillian. She's dressed in white jeans and a slim white top. And she's smiling broadly.

That's when the kitchen turns purple.

CHAPTER FIFTEEN

Lillian's Surprise

I turn around slowly. I hear the roar of the blender. I see the top of the blender sail across the kitchen. It lands in a bowl of chocolate.

A purple tornado spews from the blender. Rusty and Travis are covered in purple milk shake.

So are the ceiling, the floor, and the kitchen table.

Mom rushes into the kitchen and switches off the blender. Every kid in the kitchen is silent.

Sadora snaps photos of it all. I can see she's trying to stifle her giggles.

Sabin runs in and sees the mess. He grabs his dog and disappears in a hurry. Zero still has a piece of sliced chicken dangling from his mouth.

Mom finally speaks. "Well, I always wanted my kitchen painted purple!" She laughs so hard she almost cries.

When kids see that she is not really angry, they start to laugh as well.

"I'm sorry, Mrs. Sanford," Rusty says. "I guess I didn't put the top of the blender on tight enough."

"You think?" Mom glances at the ceiling, then at Rusty. "You're a mess, kid!"

Rusty looks down at his shirt. It used to be yellow.

"Sabin!" Mom calls. "Take Rusty and Travis up to your room and find them clean shirts. Show them the bathroom and let them get cleaned up."

"Okay, Mom." Sabin comes down to get Rusty and Travis. Zero is not with him.

Mom goes to find the mop.

All this time, Lillian is standing at the front door. Her driver stands behind her, holding a large package.

I turn to her and say with a grin, "Welcome to Sassy's Dazzle Disaster Dinner Party!"

"I'm sorry I'm late," she says.

"It's a good thing you were," I tell her. "You could have been covered with purple milk shake, too!"

"Parties without problems are no fun," she tells me. "It looks like I missed the good part."

"Actually, we're just about ready to eat. Come on in!"

She turns to the driver. "Can you set the box over there?" she asks him politely.

"Of course, Miss Ling," the driver says. He deposits the box in the family room. "I will be waiting for you outside," he tells Lillian. Then he heads back to the car.

I'm impressed.

"Lillian is here, everybody!" I announce. "And it's time to eat. At least what's left! Bring your creations to the big table here in the dining room."

The girls bring the chocolate-covered bananas. The fruit stuck on the skewers really does end up looking like bouquets of fruit flowers. The marbles worked perfectly.

"I hope the dog enjoyed the meat!" Jasmine says. She glances at the empty tray on the floor.

"There's more in the refrigerator," I tell her. "But everyone will have to get it out of the package, not off an elegant tray." I feel a little bummed out.

"It's not a problem," Jasmine says. She runs to get more bread and lunch meat. The kids don't seem to care that it's not on a tray. They have a great time cutting the cheese and bread and meat into shapes.

I walk back to the kitchen while they are making the sandwiches. Mom is still wiping up purple stuff.

"I'm sorry, Mom. I wanted it to be perfect. I'll help you clean up."

"Nonsense!" she says. "Get out those kaleidoscope fruit pizzas and wow them!"

I grin at her and take them out of the refrigerator. "Thanks, Mom!"

When I take the fruit pizzas to the table, everybody claps. I feel so proud. Sadora takes several pictures.

It's a little hard to cut the pizzas because they are sticky and gooey, but everybody gets a slice. We eat all of the first one and all but one piece of the second one.

I wrap up that piece in plastic and put it on a shelf in the kitchen. I also place several little strawberry mice, two fruit kabobs, and two chocolate-covered bananas on a plate. And some sandwiches. And set down the huge bowl of banana pudding.

"Grab a plate and eat until you pop!" I announce to all the kids.

The bubble-gum sodas are a hit. Then I realize I forgot to fix the bologna bowls! Nobody notices. Carmelita's peanut butter balls are yummy, and Travis's dirt pudding is just plain gross. But really good.

Rusty and Travis come back downstairs wearing two of Sabin's old T-shirts. They are only a little bit too big for them. They grab plates and fill them with treats.

"Oh, I almost forgot!" I tell everyone. I run to the freezer and bring out the frozen orange pie and the red Sparkle Sickles.

"More sweets!" Travis cries with glee. "Sassy, this is the best party I've ever been to!"

Everybody nods in agreement. They eat it all.

Kids laugh and giggle and tell stories about school and teachers. Everybody shares food and makes sure everyone gets to taste each item. Lillian laughs and jokes with everyone else. It's like she's a different kid from that little girl who looked so scared when she first got here.

While they are eating the pie and sucking on the Sparkle Sickles, I grab the plate I had fixed from the shelf in the kitchen. I take it upstairs and knock on Sabin's door.

"You mad at me?" he asks.

"No. Everything is okay." Zero is peeking from under Sabin's bed. "I brought you some food," I tell Sabin.

"You did?" He sits up on his bed. He looks so happy.

"Yeah. But nothing for Zero," I say with a smile. "I think he's full!" The dog slides back under the bed.

I reach into my Sassy Sack and pull out a whistle. I hand it to my brother.

"What's that for?" Sabin asks.

"Dog training!" I tell him with a laugh.

"Thanks, Sassy," Sabin says. "I'm glad your party isn't messed up."

"In spite of everything, I think it might be the best party ever," I tell Sabin.

I walk back downstairs and glance at the mess in the kitchen. I will help Mom clean up every purple spot when the kids go home.

In the dining room, everybody seems to be just about finished. I help myself to a bowl of banana pudding.

Lillian sees me come back in the room. She stands up. "I have an announcement," she says to everyone.

The crowded room gets quiet. "What's up, Lillian?" Travis says.

"First," she says, "I brought a gift for everyone."

"These aren't good-bye gifts, are they?" I ask her.

"No, I guess you can call them 'hello' gifts instead," Lillian answers.

I'm a little confused.

She opens the large box that the driver had brought in. Inside are fifteen identical small fishbowls. She pulls one out.

"Because you are my friends, I made these for you. Also because my project for Miss Armstrong is about the ocean!" she adds with a giggle.

"What is it?" Travis asks.

"Well, for starters, you can eat it," Lillian tells him. "It's just Jell-O."

"But it looks like a little ocean!" Misty says in amazement.

I look closely at the fishbowl Lillian gives to me. On the bottom I see blueberries. Swimming in the blue gelatin I can see gummy sharks and gummy fish. I can even see gummy flowers growing from the blueberry rocks.

Sadora snaps several photos of them.

"This is the coolest thing I've ever seen!" Rusty says. "I don't think I want to eat it. I don't want to mess it up!"

"Thanks, Lillian," I say. "From all of us."

Everybody nods in agreement.

"So what's your announcement?" I ask. "Please don't tell us you're moving away."

Lillian looks at all of us. "Well, I know that I'm sort of a mystery around here."

"True that," says Charles.

"I have never had the chance to make real friends before I came here," Lillian admits. "But you guys have been so nice to me."

"Go on," Princess says gently.

"My parents have been really successful in the business world. They told me they wanted me to have all the nicest things that money can buy."

"Can your folks adopt me?" Rusty asks with a grin. "Then they can buy me nice stuff, too!"

"Money can't buy friends," Lillian replies quietly. "And it can't buy a hug from your mom when she's far away."

Rusty has no reply to that.

"So where does the limo come from?" Travis asks. "We have been dying to know."

"It's supposed to keep me safe. But all it does is make me sad."

"But it's so sleek and cool!" Ricky says.

"And lonely," Lillian adds. "I would much rather be on a smelly old school bus than be by myself in a fancy car. There is nobody to talk to."

"I'll trade places with you any day!" Travis shouts.

Lillian smiles. "Well, that's part of what I want to tell everybody. Mom and Dad have sold most of their companies and will be working from home from now on. They see how happy I am here. So we are going to stay! We are moving to a regular house, right here in town."

"Awesome," I say.

Lillian looks joyous. "My mom will tuck me in each night. No more nannies. No more butlers and maids. And I get to ride the school bus, starting on Monday!"

Everybody cheers.

"That's great news!" I tell Lillian. "No more limo?"

"I have one last ride in it," she says. "And that's tonight. So they sent the big car. The stretch limo."

Misty looks out the window. "Whoa! It takes up your whole driveway, Sassy!"

"How come they sent such a big car?" Jasmine asks.

Lillian takes a deep breath. "Because I have permission to offer everybody a ride home in the limousine!"

I can hear gasps. Then whoops. Then the roar of cheers.

"For real?" Princess whispers.

"If you give the driver your address, he'll enter it into the car's GPS system," Lillian explains.

"But my mom is coming to pick me up!" Princess says.

"Let's call all the parents and see if we can get permission," Sadora suggests. "We've still got an hour."

Between cell phones and our house phone, everybody's mom or dad gets called within fifteen minutes. Every single kid gets permission to ride home in the limo!

We troop outside for more pictures. In front of the limo. Next to the limo. Inside the limo. With the uniformed driver. The boys pose with shades on. The girls strike a glamour pose. I make sure Sadora takes a photo of me with my shiny Sassy Sack slung across my chest.

Sadora takes like a zillion pictures.

"Thanks, Big Sis," I tell her. "Your pictures are going to make a dynamite slide show for my project."

"It was fun, Sassy," she says. "When everything turned purple, I rolled!"

"I bet the other kids wish they had a cool sister like you."

She gives me a big smile. "Let me know if you need help making the slide show." She goes back into the house.

The driver enters everyone's address into his machine.

"Wait a minute!" I wail. "I live here! I don't get to ride!"

Lillian laughs. "How about if we take everybody home, then bring you back here? You will be the very last one to get out. Except for me."

"Super!"

It is almost time to go. Everyone hurries to slide into the soft leather seats of the limo. Each person carefully clutches his or her fishbowl from Lillian.

Soft lights decorate the inside of the limo. Softer music plays through speakers.

"I'll be right back," I tell the kids.

I run back into the house. Mom has purple spots on both cheeks. She is looking up at the ceiling and shaking her head. Sadora snaps a picture of her.

"Mom," I say quietly.

"Yes, Sassy."

I run to her and give her a hug. "Thank you for the party. It was the best day of my life."

She squeezes me tightly. "Run along, now," she says. "We'll finish getting all the purple off tomorrow. Have fun with your friends."

I hurry out the door and into the evening. Ready for my very first ride in a stretch limousine.

Sassy's Delicious and Delightful Recipes

A note from Sassy: I want to share my yummy recipes with you. None of these requires the oven. Three need a microwave. One needs a blender — don't forget the top! You don't want to make your kitchen purple like in the story! Always work with an adult in preparing these recipes, and make sure to wash up before handling food! Be creative and add your own ingredients. Have fun!

Sassy's Red Frozen Sparkle Sickles

Ingredients

1 cup pineapple juice
1 cup red fruit punch
1 cup applesauce
½ cup crushed pineapple
¼ cup sugar
1 package Popsicle sticks

Directions

1. Mix all ingredients in a bowl.
2. Pour into ice cube trays. (A tray with fun shapes is even better!)
3. Place in freezer.
4. Add Popsicle sticks after one hour.
5. Remove when frozen and enjoy!

Sassy's Dazzling Banana Chocolate Sprinkle Delight

Ingredients

6 medium bananas
1 package Popsicle sticks
1 container chocolate ice cream topping
1 container multicolor candy sprinkles
1 bag crushed walnuts (or granola)

Directions

1. Slice bananas in half lengthwise.

2. Place on waxed paper on a plastic tray.

3. Insert a stick into one end of each banana half.

4. Place in freezer for half an hour.

5. Pour two cups chocolate topping into a deep bowl.

6. Warm bowl of chocolate topping in microwave for one minute until it is soft.

7. Place sprinkles on a flat plate.

8. Dip bananas into the warm chocolate.

9. Then roll chocolate-covered bananas in sprinkles or granola.

10. Chill until ready to serve.

Sassy's Yummy Strawberry Mice

Ingredients

10 to 15 fresh, large strawberries
1 package mini chocolate chips
1 package small almond chips
1 package red string licorice
small chunks of cheese (any kind)

Directions

1. For each strawberry, slice a piece from one side so it lies flat.
2. Press a mini chocolate chip into the pointed end of the strawberry for a nose.
3. Press two tiny pieces of chocolate into the berry to make the eyes.
4. Stick in two almond slivers for the ears.
5. Add red string licorice for the tail. (You might need a toothpick or fork to help make the hole for the tail.)
6. Serve with chunks of cheese so the mice can eat, too!

Sassy's Technicolor Fruit on a Stick

Ingredients

1 package skewers for fruit or meat (long, pointed skinny sticks)

Pick from any or all of the following fruits or add your own:
   cantaloupe
   grapes, both red and green, seedless
   honeydew
   kiwi
   lemon juice or pineapple juice
   pineapple
   strawberries (small; leave whole)

Directions

1. Wash all fruit.

2. Slice cantaloupe, honeydew, and pineapple, if using. Cut fruit other than grapes and strawberries into bite-size chunks.

3. Drizzle fruit with lemon juice or pineapple juice to prevent browning.

4. Place 6 to 7 pieces of fruit on each skewer, alternating colors, shapes, and textures.

5. Be sure to leave space at each end of the skewer for easy handling.

6. Keep the fruit sticks in a resealable plastic bag or plastic container until you are ready to serve them.

Sassy's Purple Passion Milk Shake

Ingredients

3 cups vanilla ice cream
1 cup milk
1 cup grape juice
1 cup vanilla yogurt
2 large bananas
¼ cup sugar
1½ teaspoons vanilla extract

Directions

1. Place all the ingredients in a blender.

2. Make sure the top is on tight.

3. Blend on low for one minute or until creamy.

4. Pour into clear glasses and enjoy!

Sassy's Orange Supreme Frozen Pie

Ingredients

1 cup orange-flavored yogurt
1 large container frozen nondairy whipped topping (such as Cool Whip)
1 cup canned mandarin orange slices
1 9-inch graham cracker crust

Directions

1. Combine yogurt and whipped topping in a bowl and stir.

2. Drain juice from mandarin oranges.

3. Stir oranges into mixture in bowl, setting a few slices aside for decorating.

4. Spoon into pie shell.

5. Cover with more whipped topping.

6. Decorate the top with the orange slices you set aside.

7. Cover with plastic wrap and place in freezer until ready to serve.

Sassy's Amazing Kaleidoscope No-Bake Fruit Pizza

Ingredients

2 tablespoons apricot jam
1½ teaspoons water
Pick from any or all of the following fruits or add your own:
  bananas
  blackberries
  blueberries
  kiwis
  peaches
  pineapples
  raspberries
  strawberries
1 large box graham crackers (or graham cracker crumbs)
⅓ cup butter or margarine, softened
1 8-ounce package cream cheese, softened
1 pizza pan (disposable ones are sold at lots of stores)
1 cup apple jelly, melted in microwave for 20 seconds
1 large container frozen nondairy whipped topping (such as Cool Whip)

Directions

1. Mix apricot jam with water in a small bowl.

2. Slice fruit and cut into flat, bite-size pieces.

3. Dab the fruit with the jam-and-water mixture; it will keep the fruit from turning brown.

4. Break graham crackers into pieces.

5. Place in a resealable bag and smash the crackers into tiny fragments using a rolling pin or your hands! (You can also buy graham cracker crumbs in a box, but it's not as much fun!)

6. Pour graham cracker crumbs into a bowl.

7. Add soft butter and cream cheese.

8. Mix the batter with your hands and spread it onto the pan; this is your crust.

9. Spread the apple jelly over your crust as the next layer, using a spatula.

10. Spread the whole container of nondairy whipped topping as your next layer.

11. Carefully place your fruit around the circle in a colorful, tasty pattern.

12. Cover with plastic wrap and chill until served.

Sassy's Glamorous Green Shake-a-Pudding

Ingredients

2 cups milk
1 small box vanilla instant pudding
4 to 5 drops green food coloring
1 jar with a top

Directions

1. Pour milk into jar.

2. Add instant pudding.

3. Add food coloring.

4. Put the lid on the jar and shake it, shake it, shake it!

5. Pour the pudding into small bowls and enjoy!

Sassy's Bubble-Gum Pink (or Bubble-Gum Blue) Bubbly Soda

Ingredients

1 large bottle white grape juice
4 drops red food color (or blue food color for the blue soda)
1 two-liter bottle of 7-Up (or similar product)
2 cups strawberry sherbet (or blueberry sherbet for the blue soda)

Directions

1. Add food coloring to the white grape juice.

2. Pour the juice and the soda into a large pitcher.

3. Add sherbet and serve.

Carmelita's No-Bake Peanut Butter Balls

Ingredients

1 cup crushed breakfast cereal (cornflakes or Frosted Flakes work well)
½ cup peanut butter
½ cup honey
2 tablespoons powdered milk or powdered sugar

Directions

1. Crush the cornflakes by placing them in a resealable bag and smashing them with a rolling pin or your hands.

2. Set the cornflakes aside for a moment.

3. Mix all the other ingredients together in a small bowl, using your hands.

4. Roll the peanut butter mixture into balls.

5. Roll each ball in the cornflakes until it is coated.

6. Place balls on a plate; cover plate with plastic.

7. Refrigerate until time to serve.

Travis's Dirt Pudding

Ingredients

1 box instant chocolate pudding
OR 1 carton ready-made chocolate pudding
1 package dark chocolate cookies
1 package gummy worms

Directions

1. Make the chocolate pudding according to the directions on the box.
2. Crush the cookies into teeny pieces. Use the back of a spoon or place in a resealable bag and smash them with a rolling pin or your hands! Set half aside.
3. Stir the crushed cookies into the pudding.
4. Place the dirt pudding into a large bowl.
5. Sprinkle remaining cookie crumbs over the top of the pudding.
6. Stick gummy worms into the pudding for effect.

Jasmine's Famous Creamy Banana Pudding

Ingredients

6 to 8 bananas
2¼ cups milk
1 box vanilla wafers
1 small box banana instant pudding

Directions

1. Slice the bananas into bite-size pieces.

2. Line the bottom and the sides of a large bowl with vanilla wafers.

3. Place banana slices on the bottom layer of vanilla wafers.

4. Add another layer of vanilla wafers.

5. Continue until the bowl is almost full of bananas and wafers.

6. Make the banana pudding according to the directions on the box.

7. Before it starts to set, pour the liquid pudding over the bananas and cookies.

8. Decorate the top with extra cookies.

9. Cover with plastic and refrigerate.

Lillian's Edible Fishbowl

Ingredients

2 packages blueberry gelatin
1 small clean glass fishbowl
½ cup blueberries
½ cup grapes
1 package gummy fish
1 package gummy sharks
1 package gummy flowers
1 package gummy worms
1 thick pretzel rod
1 package red string licorice

Directions

1. In a bowl, prepare gelatin according to directions on package.

2. Refrigerate for one hour.

3. While the Jell-O is gelling, add blueberries and grapes to bottom of fishbowl; these are the rocks on the bottom.

4. While it is still soft, spoon the gelatin over the fruit; this is the water.

5. Push the gummy fish, sharks, and flowers into the gelatin.

6. Place in refrigerator; serve cold.

7. To make a fishing pole, tie some red string licorice to a gummy worm, place a pretzel rod on top of the fishbowl, and attach the red string licorice to it.

Sassy's Pizza Pizzazz Bagel Sandwiches

Ingredients

6 to 10 mini bagels
1 cup spaghetti or pizza sauce of your choice
variety of sliced cheeses of your choice
sliced pepperoni or bologna

Directions

1. Cut bagels in half.

2. Spread pizza sauce on each half.

3. Cut cheese to fit and place as next layer.

4. Cut bologna to fit or add pepperoni as next layer.

5. Top with another layer of cheese.

6. Place in microwave for twenty seconds or until cheese is melted.

7. Serve immediately while still warm.

Sassy's Sizzling Bologna Bowls

Ingredients

1 package thick-sliced bologna
1 package sliced cheese

Directions

1. Place one slice of bologna on a microwavable plate.

2. Break cheese into several pieces, each the size of a half-dollar.

3. Place pieces of cheese in the center of the slice of bologna.

4. Microwave for twenty seconds.

5. As it cooks, the bologna will curve into a bowl that holds the melted cheese.

6. Serve immediately while still warm.

Sassy's Sassy Sandwiches

Ingredients

sliced bread, whole wheat or white, your choice
variety of sliced lunch meats: chicken, turkey, ham, or roast beef
an assortment of fun-shaped cookie cutters
sliced cheese, your choice
lettuce
sliced tomatoes
sliced onions
ketchup
mustard
mayonnaise

Directions

1. Choose your bread and lunch meat.

2. Choose a cookie cutter.

3. Cut your bread and meat into matching shapes, then place shaped meat on bread.

4. Stack your sandwich with your choice of lettuce, tomatoes, and/or onions.

5. Add ketchup, mustard, and/or mayonnaise for flavor and color.

6. Enjoy your custom-made, fun-shaped sandwich!

Sassy's Smart Sandwich Wraps

Ingredients

all the leftover meat from Sassy's Sassy Sandwiches
all the leftover lettuce, tomatoes, and onions from Sassy's Sassy Sandwiches
soft sandwich wraps — red or green or plain
1 bag shredded cheese (optional)
¼ cup mayonnaise or soft cream cheese

Directions

1. Chop leftover meat and cheese into very small pieces.

2. Toss everything into a mixing bowl.

3. Mix leftovers with the mayonnaise or cream cheese. Add shredded cheese if desired.

4. Place the wrap filling into the soft shells.

5. Fold the shells and serve, or refrigerate and save for later.

6. Looks ugly — tastes great!

404